MW01231682

AWAKE THE CULLERS

AMANDA YOUNG AND
RAYMOND YOUNG JR.

To all the real heroes who proceed with faith, protect the innocent and face the true monsters in our world.

ONE

Candice awoke to the smell of smoke. She blinked the sleep from her eyes. The sounds of screaming woke her the rest of the way. Hesitantly, she opened her door. Her father fought against a man twice his size. The door was broken into splinters on the ground. Beside it lay her mother, bleeding from a crushed skull she would not wake from. Her father fought with all the energy and strength of a man half his age. His eyes were full of rage, his movements fed by the need for revenge, the need to survive and the need to protect Candice from following her mother.

The stranger was a horror to behold. Blades protruded from his arms. Scar tissue surrounded the spots where they were jammed in to the skin. Her father struck him, but the man only grinned at seeing his own blood pool on the floor. With no sign of slowing down, he battered her father back. Candice saw her death then. Her father would fall, soon. She would see him die, but there would be no time to grieve. If she was lucky, it would be quick for her. If not ... well, it was out of her hands either way. She took solace in knowing she would not feel anything come tomorrow.

Then her father surprised her. Ignoring the many blades cutting into his skin, he grabbed the stranger's arms and pushed him back. Until that moment she had not noticed the fire which was fed by a fallen lantern. It covered almost the entire front wall. The stranger screamed as his armor and blades became superheated, his skin blistering around them. She was still staring at the man when her father grabbed her arm and led her through the back door. Behind their house was where they kept the horses and chickens. Coops lined the left side of the walkway from the house while a hitching post followed to the right. At the back of the yard was a small barn where the horses slept and ate. She could smell the blood from the back door. Portions of their fence were broken or missing. Chickens ran around frantically, most of their cages busted open or in pieces on the ground. As they ignored the chickens and ran to the barn, Candice heard the screams throughout the village as similar scenes played out in other homes. Thankfully, their house was at the edge of the village, so they were able to move about the yard unnoticed. There was no need to open the barn. The door hung off two broken hinges and fell to the ground the second her father touched it. The smell of death was stronger, now. Her father cursed, and she could see why. Dead and dying horses littered the ground. Only one, Sunshine, remained.

Sunshine was light with a blonde coat and hair. She bore a white star shape at the center of her forehead and was friendly and reliable. But she was a small horse, not capable of carrying two people, at least not for any distance and when speed was of the essence. Grabbing some blankets since there wasn't time to saddle the horse, her father picked her up and put her on the horse. "Head north and don't stop until you reach town."

"But that's almost three days away." She'd never ridden Sunshine that hard before. She'd never ridden any horse that hard before.

"Go." He slapped the horse to make it move and stood watching as they rode away, jumped, over the broken fence, and disappeared into the woods.

———

"I DON'T KNOW how I let you talk us into traveling south with you?" Thomas cut at the foliage to make a path.

"Because you love adventure," Kern replied, cutting at stray limbs Thomas missed. Thomas was human, one of the few full humans to ever work in the Flame Guard, an elite group of assassins and espionage agents stationed in the city of Suriax. Kern, a three-quarter elf, was also once a member of that select group. But that was long ago. Now, they would probably both be arrested if they ever stepped foot in Suriax again.

"What I'd love is to be back in the mountains introducing Marcy to my family and settling down to the quiet life of a farmer."

"Planting season is months away. You still have a little time left before you become boring," he teased.

"I happen to like boring," Thomas argued.

"Then what are you doing here?"

"Keeping you from getting into trouble," Marcy answered, pushing her way through the trees to join them.

"Marcy, my dear," Kern replied, "that is an impossible task."

"Probably," she agreed.

"You know, getting so close to your sister's territory probably isn't such a good idea." Thomas broke through to a clearing and sheathed his sword. Without preamble, he took a seat on a rock. "Who's for lunch?"

"I'll cook," Marcy answered, setting about the task.

"What's she going to do?" Kern asked, taking his own seat. "It's not like she'll even know if I do cross the border, not that I plan to. I'll be in Alerian territory the entire time. Besides, Pielere asked me to check out the rumors of those raiders traveling north. He needs to know if they should send troops down here. With it being so close to Maerishka's lands, she may consider it an act of war if they send any troops without concrete proof of danger. Things are just starting to calm down between the two cities. They don't want to stir everyone back up again."

Just a few short months earlier the cities of Suriax and Aleria were on fire, literally. Queen Maerishka of Suriax made a deal with her god, Venerith, giving up her entire city and all its people to him in exchange for power. Venerith heard her and granted the request, showering down blue fire from the sky and changing the people of Suriax, forever branding them as his own.

Aleria, led by Maerishka's half-siblings Pielere, Mirerien, and Eirae, was located just north of Suriax. The cities were only separated by a small river with protective walls lining each side. Once one city, they split a generation before and became the capitals of their own separate kingdoms. They were both founded on a strict observance of the law with one big distinction. In Suriax it was legal to kill.

Just before the night of Blue Fire, Kern learned he was actually the missing brother to the Alerian monarchs, making him a half-brother to Maerishka. This knowledge forced him and his uncle to leave Suriax and put him on Maerishka's list of least favorite people. She was still convinced he would return one day to vie for her throne. But Kern couldn't care less for her throne, or any throne for that matter. All he wanted was to be left alone.

Kern pulled his cloak tight. It was a gift from Mirerien and his brothers. They accepted him when Maerishka would have him dead. Along with his uncle, now safe under their protection in Aleria, they were his family. If they needed his help, he would do what he could to help them. The smell of cooking meat brought him back to the present. They had a good bit of daylight left. Even with this break to eat, they should make it to town before nightfall. It would be nice to sleep in a bed again, although Marcy's cooking did make sleeping on the ground a little more bearable.

True to his estimations, the sun was just beginning to dip below the horizon when they came up to the next town. Small houses dotted the countryside, gathering with more density at the edge of a lake fed by two small rivers. They waved a greeting to a couple farmers rushing to finish up their work. Spotting the inn easily for its size and boisterous sounds issuing forth, they walked that way. Men drank and played card games on the porch. Inside, people laughed and played games while others sat by the bar and loudly recounted stories from their past exploits. "You two find a table. I'll rent the rooms." Kern sank into the bar stool and waited for the waitress to make her way over to him. She had light brown hair, pulled back into a bun at the back of her head. Casually, she wiped the sweat from her brow and chatted with a patron as she poured his drink.

"What'll you have?" she asked once she made it to him.

"Three ales and two rooms," he replied.

She pulled out three mugs and started pouring, telling him the cost. Kern pulled out some coins and dropped them on the counter. "Alerian money," she commented, pocketing them quickly before handing him two keys. "What brings you this far south?"

"Looking for trouble, I guess." He shot her a grin and was rewarded by an answering grin of her own.

"Oh, there's plenty of that down here."

"Any more than usual?" he asked casually, taking a swig of his drink.

She looked around, slightly uneasy. "Not quite sure, yet. Let's just say the locals are restless."

"That so? I didn't think people around these parts were easy to spook."

"You ask a lot of questions," the man beside him said without looking his way.

"It's the only way to get answers," Kern replied easily, not about to be intimidated.

"Why do you want to know?"

"Call me curious," Kern answered. The waitress looked between them and moved quietly on to the next patron.

"Curiosity can be a dangerous thing." He turned to stare at Kern, one dead eye and a scar marring the right side of his face. His one good eye looked straight through Kern.

"Is that what happened to you," he asked, "got curious and lost an eye?" There were gasps around him. The waitress even spilled some ale on her way to pour another drink down the bar.

The man stared at him another few moments before breaking out in a grin and laughing. There was a sigh of relief all around. People began talking again, the moment of danger past. "I'm Brierand."

"Kern," he took the man's hand and then finished his ale before looking at the other two drinks. Oh well, he could always get more for Thomas and Marcy later. Taking a drink out of the second mug, he pushed the third over to Brierand, who took the mug in a single swallow.

"So," he said, wiping his mouth, "why does someone from Aleria want to know about our problems way down here?"

"Are there problems?" he asked without answering.

"You could say that. Merchants who travel south don't make it back, and the last two supply caravans never made it. Some say the plains territories have declared war on us now that they are part of Suriax. Others speak of legends long forgotten from the times of the Great Wars. I heard a man the other day say he saw a Sublinate passing through. A Sublinate! Can you believe that? No one has seen their kind this way in centuries. It seems the old warning stories have come back to haunt grown men's dreams, turning them into children searching for a mother's skirt to hide behind."

As long as there had been war, there were people who excelled at war, enjoyed it, and worshiped it. There was one group who turned war into an art form, enhancing their bodies for battle, reveling in the skill of strategy and accepting death as an inevitable by-product of the many wars always raging somewhere. They enjoyed meeting an enemy honorably and defeating him in fair combat. They called themselves the Sublinates.

As with all bands of warriors, some fell to blood lust. In the midst of battle, they moved from accepting death to taking pleasure in it. Those men believed death was the true glory of war. They reveled in pain and lived in a constant state of agitation, grafting weapons onto themselves. Most Sublinates called this way of thought a perversion. There was a schism in the group, and they fought, near to the point of extinction. For when two groups who love battle as much as they decide to fight, there is little to rein them in.

And that was that, or so the stories told. Random groups of

Sublinates popped up from time to time, though they usually followed battle, leaving normal folk to believe they were merely the stuff of legends. There were those who believed the stories existed only to warn of the dangers of blood lust and senseless killing. Even Suriaxians saw the logic of avoiding such a lifestyle.

Everyone near them seemed tenser now with the revelation of the Sublinate sighting. It was not a good omen. As far as Kern could figure, it could only mean things in the Southern Plains were about to get very dangerous, if they weren't so already, and war had very little regard for borders. Thanking Brierand for the information, Kern ordered new drinks and joined Thomas and Marcy at their table and filled them in.

"So, we are most likely looking at a war about to begin," Marcy summarized.

Thomas looked off in thought, his eyes haunted. "There's one other possibility," he said quietly, holding his mug and absentmindedly swirling the contents. "When I lived in the mountains, I met a traveler, Casther. He was the Flame Guardsman who brought me back to Suriax and helped me join the Guard." Marcy nodded, having heard this part of his story before. Kern listened silently. "It was not an easy journey to Suriax. The droughts had made many people desperate. Those leaving the farming lands for the cities, hoping for a better chance at survival, met hundreds of other people seeking the same. There weren't enough jobs or resources to feed everyone. The jails were overflowing. It was a miserable time.

"One town had a killer they couldn't catch. They hired Casther to help. The bodies were brutalized, barely recognizable. No one there was up to the challenge of dealing with a criminal of that magnitude. One night, we came upon the killer as he tore apart his last victim. I'll never forget the feral look in his eyes. All over his back were scars, most in a series of three parallel lines. Some were old and scabbed over. Others were fresh and still bleeding. I froze. Casther ran up and knocked him off the body. Impossibly, the man was still alive. He whimpered softly, in too much pain to move out of the way as they fought. The monster's attacks were completely unrestrained. I heard his bones crack and break several times as Casther landed good hits. The man would laugh and continue using the damaged limbs with no hint of pain. That fight was the only time I saw real fear in Casther's eyes. He fell and would have died, but a series of arrows flew past, impaling themselves in the monster's head and chest. Even with an arrow blinding him in one eye, he didn't stop moving until the archer lunged forward and drew his blade across the man's neck, severing the head in one clean swipe. The stranger cleaned his sword and used a booted foot to turn the headless body over on the ground. He grunted in disgust at the scars before pouring a liquid over the corpse and lighting the body on fire.

"As the fire burned, the stranger turned and would have left without a word, but Casther stopped him with a hesitant touch on his shoulder. His hood fell back, revealing a man wearing a large amount of weaponry. On his head, he wore a strange crown-like structure that protruded from his skull, as though it were a part of him. The stranger stared at Casther for a moment before calmly raising his arms to set his hood back. His hands were covered in bladed gauntlets that grew out of his arms and infused his hands. His fingers clicked against each other as he moved them. He looked over at the burning body. It was almost entirely ash. The fire was nearly extinguished, just a few smoldering bits of fabric. I asked him who he was, what that other man was. He looked me straight in the eye and said, 'Beware those who bear the triple bands.' Then he left."

"And you think he was a Sublinate?" Kern asked.

Thomas shrugged. "He fit every description I ever heard of one."

"What about the other man? You don't think he was a ..." Kern couldn't bring himself to say the word they were all thinking.

Thomas looked up from his mug, his eyes devoid of uncertainty. "He bore the bands. I know what he was."

Marcy put a hand on Thomas' arm. "What are you suggesting?"

Thomas looked down and swallowed past the lump in his throat. He forced the next words out with great difficulty. "Sublinates are drawn to war, but there were no wars anywhere near the town where I met the stranger. The only thing that could have drawn him was the reports of the brutal killings. What if the Sublinates and Cullers never ended their war? What if the reason everyone thinks the Cullers are gone is because the Sublinates strike fast and eradicate any sign of them before their madness can spread?"

No one answered.

———

"Again," Zanden ordered

Rand held out his hand to help Lynnalin stand. He cringed at the bruise forming on her face, but she didn't complain. She just took her stance and prepared for the next attack. As a dwarf, he wasn't accustomed to fighting elven women, but Zanden insisted everyone in the unit, even the mage, be able to fight. His argument was simple. They needed to work together as a team, to anticipate each other's movements and fighting techniques. Learning some basic moves and watching them practice the more complicated techniques would help her know how to better use her magic to assist them in a fight.

Conversely, they each spent time learning what spells she could cast, their range and intensity, both on their own and with augmentation from her Suriaxian fire, so they would be less likely to get in her way when a spell could prove more useful than close combat.

They were part of a four-man cinder unit, an advanced scout team being sent by Queen Maerishka to investigate the reports of raiders in the Southern Plains. Zanden was their leader and an expert fighter. Rand was a pretty good fighter himself. He didn't know any self-respecting dwarf who couldn't hold his own in a scrap, but that wasn't why he was on this mission. Rand was a marenpaie trainer. Marenpaie were special hounds bred in Suriax for combat, racing, and long-distance travel. They were exceptional animals, but not entirely accustomed to fighting in tandem with the Suriaxians' new fire abilities. This mission was as much a test of their adaptability and continued usefulness to the city as it was an opportunity to work out the kinks in the new fighting techniques Zanden spent the past month developing for the military. Lynnalin was the mage of their group. It was always good to have one of those around for long range attacks and support magic, and the group was rounded out by a member of the Flame Guard named Casther. Rand didn't know him before this mission assignment, but the past few weeks of intensive training had taught him not to underestimate the man's skills. When subtlety and precision were needed, he was their man.

Rand moved to begin the fight, but Zanden held up a hand. "This time with fire," he added. Lynnalin's eyes flinched, and Rand hesitated, but after a quick breath, she called forth her flames and nodded. Blue fire wrapped around her hands and arms, burning just above the surface of her skin. Rand called the fire to his hammer. The metal gleamed in the flickering light, reflecting the movements of the flames. After his old hammer caught fire and lost its wooden handle, he forged a new one made entirely of metal. The only drawback was the extra reverberation he felt when he hit something. Metal didn't diffuse the impact waves like wood did. Feeding the fire into his weapon, he felt the metal heat up. Swinging wide, he began his attack.

Lynnalin avoided his attacks with all the grace and dexterity of a mage. In other words, she stumbled and nearly fell three times while just barely avoiding serious injury. Her breathing quickened, and she had the wide-eyed look of someone trying to follow his movements without the skill the keep up. Then everything changed. He swung down, and she used her fire to deflect his blow. Still unsure of herself, she did not follow through with an attack of her own but jumped back and threw off two blue fireballs in quick succession to buy herself some much-needed space. Breathing heavily, she dodged his next few attacks with the confidence of someone who knew where the blow was coming from, though the grace was still lacking.

"Enough," Zanden said. They stood at rest and let their fire go out instantly. "Good," he told Lynnalin, patting her on the shoulder. "You are learning to anticipate the attacks. That's enough for today. You two get some rest. We make it to the border tomorrow."

TWO

Marcy pumped the handle to get water from the well and fill the last of the canteens. Humming to herself, she began to sing. So lost was she in the song, an old ballad on the Sublinate/Culler War, she did not hear anyone approach. The sound of clapping startled her into dropping the canteen. Water spilled out onto the ground, quickly soaked up by the dry sand around the well. A large human man stood, leaning against the outer wall of the tavern. While she eyed him suspiciously, he stepped forward and picked up the canteen, handing it back to her.

"We don't get too many elven women around here," he commented.

"I'm just passing through." She stepped to the side, edging her way past him, but he matched her steps, not giving her an easy opening to leave. A good two heads taller and broad in the chest, he towered over her. She was not completely unaccustomed to being shorter than those around her. She grew up a full elf in a city full of half-elves. Even Kern was only three-quarters elf, so he had some added height from his human heritage. But this man was tall, even for a human. His eyes looked over her appraisingly, and she felt her stomach turn.

"This can be a dangerous place for a woman such as yourself," he warned.

"I'll be fine." She moved to rush past him, but he grabbed her arm. Pulling her to him, he held her opposite shoulder with his other hand and leaned in to speak directly into her ear. His body wrapped around her like a cloak.

"Such a small thing like you needs protecting. Otherwise, someone could try to take advantage of you." He slid his hand down into the top of her blouse.

"I don't need protecting," she said defiantly, hiding her reaction to his touch.

"Oh?" he answered, clearly unconcerned with what else she may have to say. His confidence ended a moment later with her next three words.

"I'm a Suriaxian." Blue fire came to her hands, burning his arms and singeing his jacket. The man jumped back, his eyes wide with fear. Marcy fed the fire until it formed a small ball hovering just above her fingers. As she made ready to throw it, the man jumped and ran away. Marcy closed her hand and extinguished the flame. "Oh, well, time to go."

Grabbing the fallen canteens, she topped off the last one and plugged the cap in the hole. Rushing back to her room, she looked around for Thomas, but he was not around. She grabbed their travel bags off the bed and knocked next door, waiting for Kern to answer. Thomas sat looking over their map at a small table in the room. He looked up in surprise as she tossed him his bag. "We need to go."

"She's up there," a voice called from down the stairs. Several sets of footsteps walked loudly up the steps.

Kern looked over at her. "For you, I presume?" She nodded. Kern pulled her inside the room and waited with the door half-closed. Three men appeared over the stairs. The first two looked like some kind of constable or law officers. The third man looked panicked and had pretty bad burns just starting to blister on his hands. Kern shot a glance at Marcy, who shrugged.

"Can I help you?" he asked when the men stopped in front of his door.

"He's harboring the Suriaxian," the burned man shouted. One of the officers motioned him to be quiet and moved him a few steps down the hall. The other officer turned back to Kern with a serious face.

"There are claims you travel with a Suriaxian female. Is that correct?"

"Why should it matter to anyone who I travel with?"

"The woman in question was involved in an altercation with one of our citizens."

"Well, that certainly doesn't sound like her, unless she was provoked, of course." He looked pointedly at the burned man.

The officer followed his look with a grimace, not bothering to defend the man. "Be that as it may, we do not allow Suriaxians in this town. You and your companions will have to leave immediately."

"Wait, you aren't going to arrest her?" the burned man complained. "She's dangerous, a menace." The rest of his objections faded away as the officer moved him out of earshot, back down the stairs.

"Of course," Kern answered and closed the door. "I must say, Marce, your social skills are parallel to none." She grinned ruefully.

"What did he do to you?" Thomas demanded, standing angrily. Marcy's face flashed with uncertainty.

"Obviously nothing Marcy couldn't handle," Kern said.

"Those were some nice burns you gave him. Have you been practicing?"

"Some," she looked away.

"Good," he said, surprising her. When the Night of Blue Fire came, they were both affected, but Kern gave up his powers, turning his back on Venerith and forsaking his Suriaxian citizenship. Since that time, Marcy avoided talking about the fire or her own continued use of it. Whether she thought he may be jealous that she kept the power he lost, or if she felt guilty for not doing the same, he couldn't tell. Either way, it didn't matter to him. He did not want that kind of power, but he did not begrudge her for keeping it. He didn't even know if it would be possible for her to do as he did, should she wish to. The power was hers. She might as well use it. "It may come in handy in the Southern Plains."

"So, we are crossing the border?" she asked.

Thomas folded up the map and threw his bag over his shoulder. "Yes, Kern and I decided it is the best way to learn if the raiders are something more before they have a chance to make it farther north."

Kern grabbed his own bag and put his few belongings in it. Marcy handed them each a canteen, and they were off.

———

LYNNALIN SIPPED her tea and stretched out her toes. Rand and Casther sat on the other side of the fire. They were checking their weapons and supplies. Zanden stoked the flames and turned the meat over the heat. Everyone was more subdued tonight. This was the first night since crossing the border. Zanden pulled off the meat and took a bite. The fire crackled in the quiet night. Lynnalin flipped through her spell book and scrolls, taking inventory of everything she had. Some of the scrolls were a little advanced, even for her, but she felt fairly confident she could pull them off if the need arose. She organized the scrolls in order of ones she may need to access the quickest and put them back in her bag. Checking all her potions, she readied her bag for the morning. They were only two days north of the last village attacked, meaning they could run into trouble at any time. Volunteering to take the first watch, she puffed up her blanket and positioned herself to where she could see all the camp and much of the surrounding area. She hadn't cast any spells today, so it could be the last time for a while she could share in the watches. Frequent spell-casting required time to recover else she risked losing focus and miscasting or just forgetting her spells entirely. Everyone understood this, so on days when she used her magic, the others split the watches, allowing her the extra sleep she needed. But Lynnalin did not want to take advantage of her role in the group. She could pull her own weight. Sharing in the watches helped her prove that. One by one, the others fell asleep. She listened to their even breathing, drawing runes in the dirt by her leg to pass the time. In the distance, she heard night birds flying after their prey. Bushes rustled softly. Then one of the hounds woke, looking sharply to the west. She followed his gaze, straining to hear. She thought there could be voices, but her ears were not sensitive enough to tell for sure. Tapping on Casther's shoulder, she motioned to the direction of the sounds. She and Zanden were mostly elf, but Casther was full elf, which gave him the advantage of ultra-sensitive hearing. If anyone could tell what the sounds were, it would be him.

"Voices?" she mouthed. He nodded. She moved to wake Rand, and Casther woke Zanden. Together, they quietly moved in the direction of the voices. As they got closer, Lynnalin could make out a woman and at least two men talking and laughing. She scrunched her face, trying to figure out why they sounded familiar. Zanden motioned them to fan out and surround the other camp. Lynnalin and Rand took the left, while Zanden and Casther stayed right.

"I'll be right back," the woman said, walking toward Lynnalin and Rand. They took positions, preparing to attack if necessary, as the woman stepped through the trees. Lynnalin felt her jaw drop.

"Marcy!"

The smile died on Marcy's face as she turned in the direction of her name. Fire sprang to her hands. Lynnalin stepped forward, lowering her hood. "It's me."

"Lynn?" Marcy asked in shock, dropping her fire and rushing to hug her friend.

"What are you doing here?" they asked in unison.

Lynnalin was an old friend of Marcy and her brother Bryce. She often made magical items for his tavern. But Marcy left town without any warning during all the craziness a few months before. All she knew about Marcy and her whereabouts came from random snippets of information she gathered from Bryce after his infrequent updates from his sister. She still wasn't entirely sure why Marcy left. "I thought you were going to the mountains," Lynnalin said. That was the last thing Marcy told Bryce, anyway.

"Small detour," Thomas explained. Thomas, followed by Kern, joined them in the clearing. Zanden and Casther entered the clearing from the other side, taking their place by Rand.

"What are you doing here?" Marcy asked again.

"Same as us, I'd wager," Kern answered for her. "They're investigating the attacks."

"And why do three former Suriaxians care about raiders in the Southern Plains?" Zanden asked, suspiciously.

"Just doing a little recon for Aleria," Kern answered. "We

are assessing the potential threat north of the Plains." The two men eyed each other.

"Hello, Thomas," Casther said, inclining his head in greeting. Thomas looked over in surprise and inclined his head in return. The two men obviously knew each other, but they were both from the Flame Guard, so that wasn't so surprising.

Rand laughed, diffusing much of the tension, and put up his hammer. "So," he said to Kern, "you're the queen's half-brother I've heard so much about."

Kern laughed, responding to Rand's outspoken honesty. "So I am."

"It's true then?" Lynnalin said. "How did you keep it a secret for so long?"

"I didn't know until recently," he answered. "Why don't we all take a seat and compare notes? Honestly, I think we could use each other's help on this one."

"What makes you think we need your help?" Zanden challenged.

"From what we heard in the last town, I'd say you could use all the help you can get."

Before Zanden could answer, the sound of hooves hitting the ground at a rapid pace drew all their attention. They moved just as the horse and rider came crashing through the trees, running past them. The rider, a girl, squealed in surprise at seeing people. She jerked on the reigns reflexively and sent the horse tumbling in an effort to turn. The girl flew off its back, rolling into the bushes. The horse collapsed in exhaustion. Lynnalin and Marcy shared a glance and walked over to the girl, touching her softly on the leg and side. She jerked conscious and scooted away, fear in her eyes.

"Feel no fear, we mean no harm," Mary said in a sing-song voice, slipping into an old lullaby. The girl responded instantly, melting into Marcy's arms with a whimper. Marcy sang and stroked her hair.

"This horse has been ridden hard for days," Thomas said, examining the beast and giving it water from his canteen.

"Where are you from?" Lynnalin asked.

The girl, still calmed by Marcy's singing, looked up at Lynnalin. "Breakeren," she answered. Lynnalin looked back at Zanden. That was the location of the last attack. By all accounts, this girl was the only known survivor.

———

"WE ARE HERE," Zanden indicated on the map. "Breakeren is there. If we come around this way, we will get cover from the hills."

"That's assuming the raiders are still there," Kern pointed out.

"Until we know otherwise, we will act as though they are. Once we get there, we can reassess the situation based on what we find." Zanden folded up the map and put it away.

"What about her?" Lynnalin asked, motioning to the girl, still asleep on Marcy. She stayed by her side the entire night. Marcy hummed softly to her, running her fingers through her hair to keep the girl from waking frightened. They were on the opposite side of their new joint camp. The marenpaie slept along the outer perimeter. The girl's horse gave them a wide berth but didn't move too far from Thomas, who continued to provide it food and water.

"There's an Alerian town not too far north of here," Kern said. "She should be safe there."

"The problem is getting her there," Rand observed. "We need to get to Breakeren now if we hope to find anything. We don't have time to go leading some girl through the wilderness, into Alerian lands no less."

"Thomas and I can take her," Marcy volunteered, keeping her voice low to keep from waking the girl.

"That's a good idea," Kern agreed. Thomas nodded. From their Guardsman days, Kern and Thomas possessed special communication rings that allowed them to speak to one another over great distances. Kern also had a couple of teleportation scrolls he could use if they got into trouble. Besides, Marcy was the only one the girl seemed to trust, and Thomas could keep them both safe along the journey.

"In that case," Lynnalin stood and walked over to Marcy, "take this. It's a scroll for a spell to influence people's minds and make them open to suggestions. I bought it years ago without realizing the spell had to be sung. I can't carry a tune to save my life, but you may be able to use it to make someone view you as a friend instead of a threat or a target."

"Thank you." Marcy accepted the scroll and gently woke the girl, assuring her she was being taken to someplace safe. With a few words of encouragement, she and Thomas said their farewells and were off.

"We will need to double up someone if we hope to make any real time," Zanden said. "Have you ridden before?"

Kern nodded. "Once or twice, not far, though."

"Good enough. Lynnalin, you ride with Casther. Let's go."

———

DRANDER MEAT WAS a delicacy across the continent. The Farnesay gnomes domesticated the beasts hundreds of years ago. The meat was highly sought after for its rich, deep flavor and ability to complement nearly any dish. It was easy to cook, hardly ever drying. No matter where you came from or how much money you had, everyone loved drander.

As the only people to successfully tame the animals, the gnomes had a corner on the market. They were the final say on who had access to the meat. After a disagreement years before with Queen Maerishka, they forbade their meat being sold to or traded in any Suriaxian territory. With her marriage to King Alvexton, the Southern Plains became hers, and the trade restrictions now covered them as well. Most plains inhabitants couldn't care less about their king's marriage or their new ruler. It had very little to do with their daily lives. But they did miss the meat. What little bit that remained from before the union of the kingdoms was now expensive and difficult to find. Most people would rather keep it to eat than sell it, even for a good price.

But the beast next to his cage was not a domesticated drander. Evan looked through the bars and could not ignore his fear at seeing the animal so near. Wild drander were large, twice or even three times the size of their domesticated counterparts. They had long, sharp tusks protruding from their massive lower jaws. The bite force behind those jaws was enough to snap a leg in two. Between the tusks sat two pair of sharp, pointed teeth with serrated edges. The rest of the mouth was full of strong molars designed to grind their food into dust before they even swallowed. They had short, hoofed legs and a bony structure going down their back. The hard bone protected their spine and made them very difficult to injure in a struggle. This shield bone branched out into several smaller bones, resembling a reversed set of ribs. All were covered by hair and visible only as lumps under the skin. A long mane of hair hid the exposed parts of their necks and throats, protecting them even further.

Evan watched the monstrous beast pull against his chain, held by a giant of a man. The man was as terrifying as the beast. Muscles bulged, practically breaking his skin. Bones, that looked strikingly similar to a drander, surrounded one arm like a bracer. The tips of the bone were shoved into the skin, held in place in some spots by metal brackets bent and bolted into the skin. His shoes and clothes were made of drander hide. All he needed was a set of tusks to complete the look.

"Is that him?" a high-pitched voice asked. Evan looked over at a girl standing outside his cage. No, not a girl. Despite her childlike height and hair pulled up in three bushy ponytails on both side and the top of her head, he could tell she was no child. Given her proportionate features and size, he would guess she must be a halfling, though he'd never actually seen one before. His village was all human with very few visitors from outside. The occasional merchant who passed through was usually human. Every five or ten years, an elf or dwarf would run the deliveries. That was rare enough to spark conversations for weeks.

The girl leaned in toward his cage and cocked her head to each side to get a better look. "Are you sure he is the one? Doesn't look like much."

"Neither do you," Evan said out of bravery or stupidity. He wasn't sure which.

Her eyes snapped toward him, and she moved. He felt a sudden pain on the side of his neck, in the soft skin just to the side of his throat. He jerked back and was held firmly in place by a small hand on the opposite side of his head. The girl's other hand held a dagger at his throat. She leaned against his back, her face pressed up against his hair. The door of his cage clanged against the metal bars as it hit the wall and then slammed back shut. Evan felt her breath down the back of his neck as she opened her mouth to speak. "To the pit," she called. The man with the drander looked up and grinned. Evan felt his skin go cold. Somehow his situation had just gotten worse. The girl pulled the knife back and returned it to a leg sheath. Walking casually to the door of the cage, she turned her back on him with no fear of attack. She walked out of the cage, leaving the door open behind her as she talked to the man.

Evan looked at his chance of escape and wondered what game they were playing. Of course, he doubted he could make it past either the girl or the giant man. They would cut him down the second he stepped foot past the bars. Even if he did somehow manage to sneak by unnoticed, there was still the drander to contend with. Evan looked at the beast and almost wished they would close the door. He wasn't getting out of here alive. The illusion of freedom was actually crueler than the cage.

The giant pulled on the chain for the drander and led him away. The girl looked back at Evan with a glint in her eye. "Aren't you coming?" she asked sweetly. Her hair shimmered in the sun, almost seeming to change from brown to red.

Evan stood and walked slowly to the door, pausing before stepping out of the cage. His stomach twisted, made worse by what he saw as they crossed the yard. Men, monsters of every size and race filled a camp the size of a small town. Some cleaned weapons or worked on other mundane tasks, made strange by the mutilated forms of the men. Every man bore a combination of various scars, missing limbs, some with weapons shoved in where the limbs once were. Their clothes were mostly tattered and bloody. Some blood was old. Some was not. There were even a few more drander scattered about, though none were as large as the first one he saw.

As they continued to walk, one man stabbed another with his sword and used the distraction to slice off the injured man's arm with a small scimitar. With a foot on the man's chest, the first man withdrew the sword and picked up the severed arm. A gleam in his eye, he removed the spiked bracer on the arm and put it on. The injured man looked down at the bleeding stump and roared in outrage, jumping on his attacker. None of this seemed to faze the halfling girl who continued walking at her same brisk speed around a corner and down, deeper into the camp.

Evan hurried to catch up, not wanting to become separated and find himself alone in this crowd. As Evan took the turn, he could see the two men still locked in their bitter battle. Those in the crowd either cheered them on or ignored the fight. Evan shook his head and tried to find the girl. Panic filled him. The crowd was thick with men, large and small, tall and wide, armed, scarred and able to kill him with very little thought or effort. Sure, he killed three of them, but that was in the heat of battle, consumed by grief for his wife and the need to protect his daughter in order to give her a good chance to escape. He was no warrior. Just when his mind threatened to focus on his fear and worry over what had become of his daughter, the halfling girl came into sight. Jumping high above the heads of the crowd, she grabbed on to the wooden frame of a wall, angled out to set off an arena of some kind. Swinging her body through the small holes between the slats, she gracefully and easily came to a perch on the top of the wall. The fabric of her pants shifted to show strong, muscular legs. The pants, slit down the sides, were secured in two spots with pins. A belt hung over the pants, holding a curved blade. The one she pulled on him before was barely visible, secured to her leg, under her pants. The open side seam allowed her quick access without making the blade completely obvious.

With a grin, she launched herself into the air, somersaulting down to the center of the arena. The men in the street crowded around the wall, eager to see what she would do. Ignoring the two men fighting in the arena, she walked over to a woman seated on a large rock and watching the fight. The girl jumped up on the rock and whispered in the woman's ear. She sat up straighter and tilted her head. Evan couldn't see her eyes under the small top hat she wore, but the shiver Evan felt made him fairly certain he was the focus of her attention. The woman stood, her short straight hair peeking out from under her hat. Her coat fanned out, large cuffs adorned with gold buttons. She had a flair about her that spoke of someone accustomed to being the center of attention. She lifted a hand, and everyone within sight fell immediately silent. The woman looked up at Evan, and he caught a glance of a small conch shell hanging on a chain around her neck.

She shifted her gaze and spoke. *"Gentlemen,"* she said, *"we have something special planned for this evening."* Evan jumped. Her lips remained still though her voice was clear and concise. Without yelling, her words reached the farthest man, seeming to come from every direction at once. *"Today,"* she continued, "we *have an initiation."* The men roared, clanging together objects and making a loud racket. The woman grinned, letting them get worked up. Tilting her head, she looked up at Evan and grinned even more. Still looking at him, she raised a hand for silence and continued. *"Who will volunteer to take to the pit and educate our new recruit in our ways?"*

Several men yelled out, fighting over each other to be selected. Evan took a step back. Her eyes continued to follow him. Turning, he stumbled through the crowd. He looked back for a brief second and came up short to find the halfling girl blocking his path.

One hand on her hip, she wagged her finger at him and clicked her tongue. "Now, now, where do you think you're going?"

Evan froze, no sounds coming from his mouth, as much as he tried to say something, anything. She stepped forward, and he stepped back. They continued their dance until he felt a wall behind his back. His hands grasped the metal rods making up the arena fence. He closed his eyes, trying to drown out the cheering and excitement of the crowd. The girl jumped onto the wall beside him and spoke into his ear. "Wake up. It's time to play. You should open your eyes. You'll want to remember this ... or not. But either way, it will make survival easier and make for a better show ... for us anyway." Giggling, she pulled on a pin from the wall, and he felt the support at his back give way. Flailing uselessly, he fell. The ground came at him hard, knocking the wind from his lungs.

"*This man,*" the announcer woman continued, "*killed three of our men during the last raid. Let's see if he can repeat that task.*"

Evan heard the whistle of something moving quickly through the air and opened his eyes to see a man swinging a battle hammer in circles to either side of his body. Evan rolled just before the hammer came down on the ground. Coming to his feet, he flinched at the pain in his back and arm.

"*Let the pain make you stronger,*" the woman's voice said softly into his ear. He shook off her words and dodged the man with the hammer, or he tried to. The hammer came down on his good shoulder with a painful crack that left it bruised and disjointed. He saw the rapture in the man's eyes as he prepared to deliver the final blow. It was the same face he saw that night. The features were different, the hair another color. This man was shorter with a more rounded jaw. But the eyes were the same. He saw that man who cut down his wife. He saw the other two men, each directly responsible for the death of a close friend. They all had those same eyes. Roaring, Evan ducked his head and rammed the man in his stomach, using the force to pop his shoulder back into place. Surprised, the man fell back, dropping his hammer. Ignoring the pain in his arm, no, not ignoring, instead letting the pain feed his actions, Evan grabbed the hammer and swung. He caught the man under the jaw with a sickening pop. The man's eyes rolled back into his head and closed.

Evan didn't have time to think of what he had done as another man came running to his side, picking him up off his feet with the momentum, and slammed Evan into the ground. This new opponent was small and covered in blades. Sharp, talon-like finger blades scratched and tore at Evan's skin. Evan pushed him off, but the man spun, slashed and kicked like a wild animal. His movements were impossible to predict. Blades on his hands, knees, and feet cut at Evan repeatedly until he dripped a trail of blood. He swung the hammer, but the man was too quick. He couldn't get close without getting cut.

After another series of slashes that left Evan woozy from the blood loss, he gave up trying to avoid injury and went on the attack. The man was fast, but there was some advantage to not caring about the outcome. Either he would win and survive, or he would die, and this would all be over. With that in mind, Evan embraced what could be his last few moments of life. His senses grew sharper. He could smell the blood and sweat. He felt the sun beat down on his skin. His shadow formed strange shapes as he moved and swung the hammer. He heard the crack of bones breaking as his weapon finally hit. Following up with more attacks, he refused to give the other man the space to recover. He may die this day, but he would take as many of them with him as he could. The man's finger blades pierced the skin of Evan's bruised shoulder. Evan just raised a knee into the man's stomach and followed with a wide swing at his head. Evan looked down at the blood on his hands, just like that night. The only difference was this time the blood belonged to him instead of the men he killed. He closed his hands and felt the blood squish between his fingers. Then the next man jumped into the arena, and he had no more time for thought.

Fighting and killing. That was his existence, now. The dirt at his feet flew in the flurry of battle. His heightened senses and screaming pain made every moment surreal. As the third man lay dead, the fourth on his way to join the fight, Evan noted, not without a hint of satisfaction, how easy it was becoming for him to kill. These men, brutes though they were, each fell to his hammer.

Standing over his latest kill, Evan looked around for his next opponent. No one moved. At the center of the arena stood the halfling girl. Her hair was blue now. Or was it purple? Evan's grip on his hammer tightened. He wanted to crush her small skull and watch that playful grin die on her face. He ran toward her, but she stood, casually picking something from her fingernails. He swung his weapon, but she jumped, briefly touching off the end of his moving hammer and somersaulting over his head. He turned, but she slid between his feet and kicked him in the back. Evan growled and tried, unsuccessfully to land a blow. She was fast and small, much more so than his second opponent. And she was barely trying to fight. Her weapons were not drawn. She didn't even use her hands to hit him. Other than the occasional kick, she didn't touch him at all.

"What's the matter?" she quipped. "Can't beat an unarmed girl?"

"*I think he's had enough for today,*" the announcer woman said. There were a few disgruntled moans throughout the crowd, but no one argued. The girl relaxed her pose, turning to face the woman, and Evan saw his shot. Running full speed the few feet between them, he swung hard. The woman in the top hat pulled out a small baton from her coat and shook it down into a long staff, catching him square in the chest and sweeping his legs out from under him. Putting one foot on his chest and pushing on the nerve in his wrist so he let go of the hammer, the woman leaned down and looked him in the eyes. "*I said, that's*

AMANDA YOUNG & RAYMOND YOUNG JR.

enough." He opened his lips, but she put a finger to them and shook her head. *"Shhh, not a whisper."*

Evan would have argued, but the combination of her hit to his chest, lying still on the ground, and too much blood loss finally took its toll, and he slipped off to blissful unconsciousness.

THREE

KERN LOADED ANOTHER BODY ON TO THE PYRE AND
headed back to search more houses. At least what was left of
the houses. This was how the entire morning had gone. There
were too many bodies to bury, so they built a pyre. That left
them each with the grisly task of carrying the dead. Lynnalin
helped where she could, but they could all see the toil it had on
her. The last house she explored was a bad one. None of them
were ready to see so much death. Even coming from Suriax,
where death was common and murder accepted, this was
different. These bodies were brutalized. Some were missing
limbs or even heads. Many were far too young. Even Suriaxians
had a soft spot for children. Whoever these raiders were, they
didn't care who they hurt.

Taking out a canteen and handing it to Lynnalin, Kern
leaned on a wall and took a few much-needed breaths. She took
the water gratefully and sighed. "You okay, Lynn?" She
nodded. "You know, no one would think less of you if you need
to take a break, go for a walk or something."

Lynnalin looked at the growing mound of bodies in the pile

and handed him back the canteen. "Thanks, I might do that ... for a few minutes," she hastened to add. Kern nodded his understanding. "Maybe after this ..." she started, but stopped, turning her head to the side. "Did you hear something?"

Kern struggled to listen but couldn't hear anything out of the ordinary. "Like what?"

"It was some kind of creaking, and I thought I heard a moan." Lynnalin tilted her head to the side as she searched, following the sounds only she seemed able to hear. With both arms, she pulled at the rubble of the door frame, trying to clear a path inside. Kern hurried to help her before she could bring down the house on her head. Practically glowing with excitement, she was oblivious to her own danger. As they moved through the house, she moved with increasing certainty. Just when Kern was about to turn around and get the others, convinced she had finally lost her mind, he heard it, too. It was faint, but he thought he heard movement below their feet, under the floor. Falling to her knees, Lynnalin threw off rugs and broken furniture, hastily searching for the door she knew she would find. "There!" she pointed to a large armoire on its side. Together, they moved it aside and revealed the trap door in the floor below it. Lynnalin pulled open the latch before Kern could recommend caution.

At first, all they saw was darkness. Steps led down into the gloomy undercarriages of the home. All was silent. "Hello," Lynnalin called. "Is anyone down there?"

No one answered, but they could hear breathing and shuffling, followed by a quiet, "Shhh!"

"Lioceretien," Lynnalin said, creating a dim ball of light that fell slowly from her hands to float down into the darkness. Children sat huddled, held by women who stared, frightened, yet defiant. "There's dozens of them," she whispered, as the light moved around to illuminate all the faces.

Kern thought to lead them out, but the smell of burning flesh caught his nose, and he looked again to all the young faces. "Keep them in the house," he cautioned. "I'll be right back. He made his way quickly to the pile of bodies, beginning to smoke from small fires burning around the outer edges. "We found survivors," he called. Zanden and the others immediately stopped their work. "Children," he added, nodding pointedly to the pile of dead. Catching his meaning, Casther grabbed some blankets and quickly smothered the fires.

"Grab some clean blankets and follow us," Zanden instructed Casther and Rand. "Lead the way," he motioned to Kern. One at a time they took the children, wrapping them in blankets and shielding their faces, and carried them quickly to their camp outside the village. Once at camp, Lynnalin distracted the children with some simple prestidigitation spells. With lights dancing over the camp and children laughing for the first time in days, everyone settled in to get a good night's sleep. The rest of the work could wait until tomorrow.

———

EVAN LET THE HAMMER FLY, crushing in his opponent's skull and watching the body fall, limp. He looked around for the next person to kill. This was how his days went now. They would throw him into the arena, hungry and tired. He would fight for his life, killing whoever they sent against him. He'd fight until they told him to stop. Then he would eat, rest, and begin again. He didn't even know how much time had passed.

He moved the hammer from hand to hand and adjusted his stance. They let him keep the hammer from his first arena kill. Funny, he always thought he would go for a sword, but the hammer fit his hands like it belonged there. He saw the next man enter and paused. He was not like the others. This man was no fighter. He was a scared, bruised and weak man, probably from some village they raided. What was this? He wanted a fighter to kill. He enjoyed killing these monsters. It felt like he did a service to the world by ending their lives. All the chaos they brought, and he had the power to end them. It was freeing, exciting, and he was getting good at it. What good was there in killing this helpless man? So pathetic, he probably hadn't even killed a single raider. Evan raised his hammer, and the man cringed. He didn't even move to grab a weapon or defend himself. Evan sneered. What good was there in letting such a useless man live? There was none. This man would die today a coward, for no reason or purpose. His life was for no purpose. The man sobbed, hands covering his face. Evan swung the hammer and ended the man without a moment's hesitation. Head caved in, hands crushed by the blow, the man fell to the ground. Evan felt nothing. That man, now a broken pile of bones and blood, was nothing to him. They all would die. How or when did not matter. He would die, too, probably with a sword in the gut or with his own skull crushed in. Evan looked down at the unbroken bones and felt the urge to break them all to pieces. Swinging his hammer, he hit anywhere that looked solid, hearing the satisfying crunch and snap of bones detaching and falling apart. He stomped on the flesh until it mixed with the dirt. Huffing, heart pounding, he heard a sound behind him and swung the hammer. The halfling girl did a back bend to avoid his strike and came up on her hands, catching his arm in her strong legs. She twisted and flipped him to his back, coming around to sit on his chest. The sun glinted off orange highlights in her bright blue hair.

In the distance, he heard men cheering and hollering as they headed off to raid another village. Random groups of men went off almost daily to loot and kill whoever happened to be nearby. There was no order to it. Men left and returned on their own, as they felt the need to kill something. Meanwhile, the majority moved with the camp, traveling gradually north. Evan heard their cheers and longed to join them. He was tired of the camp. He wanted new people to kill.

The woman in the top hat walked up to them. The girl looked up from her perch on his chest. "I'd say he is ready." She bounded off him and dusted off her pants.

"*Not quite yet,*" the woman answered. Still, she did not move her lips. "*But soon.*" He felt a thrill run down his spine. Soon.

———

It was difficult to say how long the fire burned. The sky was gray, the sun hidden behind the smoke and ash. Kern could not tell if it was midday or later. He sniffed, his nose and throat dry and scratchy. He blew his nose on a handkerchief and came away with black, crusty mucus. Turning the handkerchief inside out, he wrapped it around his face. It only helped a little. His throat cried out for water, but his canteen had been empty a long time. Only drops remained. If any of them had experience with pyres, this would be a much easier task. As it was the fire kept going out in spots, requiring them to stoke the smoldering flames, add kindling and shift the bodies to speed up the process. None of them wanted to leave this task half done for someone else to happen upon and witness the terrible truth of what occurred here.

Kern wiped the sweat from his neck. His shirt was sticky and uncomfortable against his skin. They had all long since removed their heavier armor in favor of the freedom of movement and cooler, looser clothing underneath. Kern stretched his back and cracked his neck, freezing mid-stretch. A man stood at the edge of the forest. Clad in weapons and armor, he stood watching them. Kern looked around and realized the man was not alone. Dozens of other figures watched from the forest. They were everywhere, surrounding the village on at least three sides.

Seeing Kern's change in posture and attention, Zanden stopped and looked around, taking in their change in situation. They shared a look and nodded. Kern cleared his throat to get Casther's attention while Zanden took care of letting Rand know. They did not bother going for their armor. The ambushers would be on them before they had time to don anything. Even though their main weapons were also removed from their persons, each man carried secondary, backup weapons. If it came down to a fight, it would be a good one.

The man Kern saw first raised an arm and motioned to be followed. Three men stepped from their cover of the trees. Together, the men walked toward the pyre. They held their arms at their sides, their swords sheathed, but they were not what one could call unarmed. Protrusions of bone, merged in places with shining spots of metal, snaked around their arms, forming spikes and claws. For two of the men, the spikes continued to their shoulders. The leader had bones growing through his skull to form a natural helmet. Kern knew, even without Casther's whispered word, who he now faced. "Sublinates."

The three men spread out, surveying the bodies and damage to the town. The leader continued forward. "How long?" he called back to his men.

"Four or five days," one man answered, lifting an unburned arm from one of the bodies.

"They are traveling north," another man answered, examining tracks at the edge of the clearing.

Kern's heart stuck in his throat. If they went north, that could put them on path to Thomas and Marcy. He thought of that town ravaged and plundered, a hollow shell, devoid of life, death everywhere. The man stopped in front of Kern and Zanden. His gaze shifted between the two men uncertainly. "Which one of you is in charge here?" he asked at last.

They shared a look, Zanden answering. "We are here separately, representing Suriaxian and Alerian interests in these matters."

The man nodded. "You should return to your homes."

"And ignore what those monsters did?" Rand asked angrily.

"That is why we are here, to put an end to these activities."

"With all due respect," Kern said, removing the handkerchief from his face, "we have a right to defend our people."

"Do you know what it is you face?" he eyed Kern speculatively. "I know you do," he said, looking to Casther. "This is not your first encounter. As I recall, you were somewhat outmatched on that occasion."

Casther stiffened. "That was many years ago."

"So it was. And yet, you still have not learned to stay out of these matters."

"Why should we trust you to handle things any better?" Kern asked, bringing the man's attention back to him. "Your guys enjoy war as much as they do. If we leave you to just go after and kill each other, who keeps our people from becoming random casualties in the process? You couldn't save this town, or any of the others that preceded it. It seems you are five days late and have a pile of dead farmers and merchants to show for your troubles. Do you even care about the men they slaughtered, about the children who will be haunted with these memories for the rest of their lives?"

"There were survivors?" The surprise was evident in his voice.

"Not for lack of their trying," Rand snorted. "A group of women and children hid in the basement of a home."

The Sublinates came back together, exchanging looks and a few whispered words. The leader dismissed them, and the two men rejoined the others in the woods. Try as he might, Kern still couldn't make out any details of the other men. Their leader turned back to face Kern.

"Do as you like, but don't get in our way." He walked back to the woods without a second glance back.

FOUR

"I think you're overreacting. They've got more important things to worry about than you being a Suriaxian."

Marcy shrugged and looked out over the horizon. Thomas was right, of course. As soon as word of Candace and her experiences with the raiders spread through the town, the tone of the village changed. Anxiety turned to real fear. Preparations were made. Contingencies were discussed. There was even talk of evacuating to the Eastern Ridge, a strip of mountains separating Alerian and Suriaxian lands north of the Southern Plains. And Marcy couldn't stop looking at the horizon. A sense of real fear lodged itself in her stomach and wouldn't ease up. That was the real reason she wanted to leave. Something bad was about to happen. She could feel it.

"Everything will be fine," Thomas continued. "We'll just wait here for word from Kern," Thomas paused and looked down at his hand. "That's him, now." Thomas walked back down the hill and turned his ring, initiating contact with Kern's matching communication ring. Marcy ignored him and leaned against the large tree at the top of the hill. All things considered, this was a peaceful spot, just at the edge of town, resting by the river. The sound of birds singing and water moving was louder than the bustle and conversations going on a few hundred feet away. She could almost quiet her uneasy mind and enjoy the moment. Then the birds went quiet. Marcy tightened her grip on the tree, bark coming off in her hand as the first shadows dotted the horizon. "Thomas," she said weakly, but he did not hear. "Thomas!" she said louder. He glanced her way but held up a finger and continued speaking through the ring. "THOMAS!" she practically screamed, finally getting his full attention. He turned off the ring and hurried back up the hill.

"What is it?" he asked before falling silent. The shadows had become hundreds of men, some on foot, some riding animals, all holding weapons aloft as they ran full speed toward the town. After a second look, Marcy could see that some of the weapons were actually attached and coming out of their arms, or in place of arms. "They're here," she whispered.

Thomas snapped out of his shock and pulled her down the hill. "Grab as many people as you can and head to the tavern. It's the most defensible building here. Go straight there. No detours."

"Where are you going?"

"I'll take the long way, so we can warn as many people as possible. The way they are moving, we don't have long. Go."

And she did. Marcy ran, knocking on doors and calling out warnings to everyone she saw. Some followed. Others ignored her, shrugging off her hands or slamming their door in her face. As others saw the approaching tide of fighters, word spread like a wildfire. The town bell tolled out a warning, and the scene quickly devolved into chaos. She yelled to those running by to head to the tavern, but most ignored her and kept running to their own destination. She heard screams, followed by the clang of metal and the pounding of hooves and knew they were out of time.

"Help me!" a woman cried frantically. A vegetable cart had tipped over and caught the woman's leg, pinning her in place. Marcy hesitated. She wasn't strong, and the raiders could be on them at any moment. She looked longingly at the tavern, just fifty feet away. The woman's terrified face as she lay ignored, left to die helpless and alone, did Marcy in. She lifted the end of the cart, but she was only able to move it a few inches. She and the woman pushed and lifted. Marcy threw off fruit and vegetables left in the cart, and they tried again. The sound of hooves hitting stone grew louder. It was followed by a snort that made her blood run cold. Standing a mere twenty feet away, staring straight at them, was a man riding a wild drander. The beast bore large tusks, long hair, and fangs and a bony armor that made it nearly unstoppable. His rider was no less impressive or terrifying. He wore thickly scaled bracers with spikes that seemed to pin the armor to his skin. Shards of metal poked out from under his fingernails and the gum line around his teeth. Spikes were bolted through the skin above his eyebrows and cheekbones.

Marcy felt her palms burn and let go of the cart gently. Once free, her hands burst into bright blue flames. It only seemed to excite the man more. The drander, however, was another matter. He eyed her nervously, pounding his hooves against the stone. They were at a standstill for what felt like minutes, although she knew only a second or two passed before she saw his muscles twitch. Feeding her fire, she pushed it out, bringing a wall of flames between them. The man would have continued, but the beast was too afraid to run through the fire. He yelled at the animal, but it would not budge. Angered, he stabbed a sword into the throat of the drander and dismounted, leaving the animal to his painful death. The man grinned at her and walked toward the flames.

Calling forth more blue fire, Marcy threw the small fire-balls at his head and clothes, hoping to catch them on fire. Though not much compared to a wizard's fireball, they were nothing to scoff at. He dodged a few but took most head-on. His clothes burned at the shoulder and chest. He absentmindedly patted his clothes and walked directly into the flames, emerging a burning behemoth of muscle and might. He raised the morning star from his back. The sword was still embedded in the throat of the now dead drander.

Lifting his weapon to swing, he did not expect the kick that caught him square in the head. Thomas, jumping from the roof of a nearby shed, landed his shot and followed with a sword to the gut. The man laughed. Thomas took a hard punch to the face and reeled back. Undaunted, he fought off the monster, blocking weapon swings and cutting his opponent whenever possible. Knowing he would not be able to outlast the monster, Thomas aimed for the face and head. An injured arm or gut wound would not slow him down. That left decapitation or a severe head injury. Ducking under the swing of the morning star, Thomas jumped off the side of a wall and struck down with his blade, cutting straight through to come out the man's throat. The attacker dropped the morning star and fell to the ground. Thomas pulled his sword and came to Marcy's side, lifting the vegetable cart off the woman. Marcy helped her up, and the three of them ran to the tavern. The door slammed and bolted behind them. No one else would be let inside.

Raiders filled the streets, cutting down people at every corner. The scene in the tavern was not much better. People ran around, screaming and yelling questions, cries of fear and loss, wails of hopelessness and despair. Thomas grabbed Marcy's hand and ran upstairs, attempting to instruct people to fire from the windows. No one could hear him. Marcy held on tight, but the crowd pushed in around her, and soon their hands slipped apart. She felt herself moved by the crowd, further and further away from him. Thomas turned and looked for her, frantically pushing his way through the mass of people, but they would not cooperate. Marcy felt the railing at her back. There were more jabs and pushes, bodies bumping and pressing against her. She struggled in vain to move away from the edge. She didn't hear the wood break, but she felt the moment its support was gone. For a moment, she felt relief at being away from the crowd. Then she remembered she was falling and heard herself scream.

The room fell into silence, a moment frozen in time. She felt her body supported, as if by a pillow of air. She thought she would be crashing into the floor. Instead, her body slowly floated to the ground. Through the surprised stares and still people, she saw Thomas pushing his way down the stairs to the spot where her feet softly touched down.

"Are you hurt?" His hands ran over her arms and face, checking for injury.

"I'm fine," she answered him, uncomfortable with being the center of so much attention. Over the silent tavern, the sounds of screams from outside began to bring back the severity of their situation and take precedence over everyone's shock at her fall without injury.

"Everyone," Thomas called, taking advantage of their attention while he held it. "I know this situation is bleak, but we are not without ability to defend ourselves."

"How?" someone yelled.

"They cannot die," another called. Others murmured their agreements.

"They can, and the stranger has proven so," the woman

from the vegetable cart said. "I saw him kill one of them. These two people saved my life at the risk of their own."

Bolstered by her support, Thomas continued. "We can defend this building. Support will come. We just need to hold on until it can get here. Anyone with a bow, get to the second-floor windows and start picking them off. Aim for the heads and eyes. Either you'll kill them or blind them.

"Everyone else, gather what weapons and supplies we have. We need to know what our resources are so we can see where we stand. If you have experience fighting, meet me by the bar."

Thomas began organizing the people. Marcy couldn't help staring at the broken banister. How had she survived? Her hand fell on her broach, and Marcy stopped, suddenly understanding what happened. She wore a butterfly broach made of sapphire and onyx. It was a birthday gift a few months back from Lynnalin. Lynn said there were enchantments on it, though even she did not know which ones. It was a test object from her academy training. The metal setting and gems were cool to the touch, but she could still feel the power pulsing under her fingertips. What other surprises did this broach hold?

She didn't have time to wonder about that for long. The walls shook with the force of men and weapons crashing into it. Thomas ran to the door with several men. Together, they kept the door from coming loose from its hinges. They yelled out commands to other men nearby. Those not involved in protecting the door either stood back in fear or quietly prayed for help. Marcy felt apart from the crowd. Her fear from before was gone. A new energy surged through her blood. Out of nowhere, a song came to her, and Marcy began to sing.

> They fought the fight,
> Fought for what is right,
> Defended kin and neighbor,

Survived the night,
Oh, what a sight,
The men of Valenkeeper.

The dark descent,
Of evil men,
None thought could be repelled.
How could they stand
Against such odds
And not be themselves felled?

Five hundred foe
Against but ten
Stood no match, in the end.
For when you fight
On side of light
The darkness cannot win.

THOSE WHO WERE frightened moments before were now singing boisterously along with the "Ballad of Valenkeeper." The song spoke of a group of farmers who fought a goblin attack in the small mountain settlement generations before. With limited weapons and fighting skills, the men held off the attacks for three days, until reinforcements could come to drive off the remaining goblins. It was a song of perseverance and hope that everyone learned as a child, and singing it had the desired effect of calming the fears of those in the tavern and encouraging them not to give up. Leaving them to continue singing, Marcy ran to the second floor and peaked out a window to see what they faced. It reminded her of the descriptions she heard of Suriax after the Night of Blue Fire.

Homes burned. Bodies littered the streets. The source of the destruction, however, was quite different. Raiders were everywhere, hacking at anyone unlucky enough to be caught outside. They broke in doors and pulled screaming women from their homes. They took turns cutting off limbs until their victims stopped screaming. Some lasted longer than others.

Marcy looked at the horrified, haunted expressions of the archers stationed at each window. The building shook again, and she looked down at the men running into the tavern door. The archers tried shooting at them, but none could get a good shot. Marcy raised her hands in front of her chest and called the fire. Concentrating on the flame, she grew it into a dense, tight ball. She felt the heat on her face and knew it was ready. Pushing out, she sent the fire down, focusing it on the men. They ignored it at first, but she kept the fire coming, forcing it to grow hotter.

Their hair burned down to the scalp. Skin blistered, and still they did not scream. One man threw an axe at her window. Marcy ducked but did not stop. As skin melted off their faces and the fire's heat reached their brains, at last the men fell. She thought to rest a moment, but others were quick to take their place, so she continued pumping a steady stream of fire. She maintained the fire for so long, at such intense heat that her own hands began to blister. She took in a deep breath and felt her vision blur. There was not enough air left around her to breath. The fire consumed everything. Her vision reduced to small pinpricks of light and fuzzy colors. Five more men fell to her flames. With the immediate threat reduced, Marcy let the fire extinguish, but not before her vision blackened entirely. She felt hands at her back. They kept her steady. Her air returned, and with it, her vision.

"Are you alright?" One of the archers asked. He was the

same person who kept her standing when she would have fallen. She nodded, her throat too dry to speak.

"Let me see that." A woman ran up with salves and bandages, intent on tending to Marcy's hands. They were worse than she thought. Clear, fluid-filled bubbles covered her fingers and palms. The pain as the woman cleaned and covered them was intense, but she did not flinch. She was raised in Suriax. Suriaxians often engaged in a battle of wills called *proelignisium*. The premise was simple. You cause your rival pain through fire. They do the same to you, and the first person to give up loses. Every Suriaxian participated in at least one or two *proelignis* matches in their lifetimes.

"Hey, Marce, that was good thinking." Thomas came into the room. The smile died on his face. "You're hurt!"

"I'm fine. Just a few blisters is all."

"That has never happened before."

Marcy shrugged. "I never kept it going so long before."

A loud crash sounded at the back of the tavern. It was followed by screams and people shouting. Marcy and Thomas ran to the top of the stairs. Light streamed in from holes in the back wall. Others quickly joined it as someone used an axe to break through. Thomas ran down the stairs, calling out orders. "Get all the children upstairs. Pull those tables over here. Men with weapons go over there." In less than thirty seconds, they had any large furniture they could find stacked to the left of where the raider would burst through. It was all part of their effort to funnel the enemy away from the stairs and straight for their ambush. Marcy ushered all the children upstairs, biding them to be quiet. Candace was at the head of the group, grabbing on to Marcy's arm and not letting go. She took her charges to the farthest room at the end of the hall. It had a window that overlooked the next building. The gap was narrow. If it became necessary, two adults could hand over the children from one building to the next. It wasn't a great plan, for she had no idea what awaited them over there, but it was an option.

Singing softly, she did her best to calm the frightened children. She sang a song of a jovial gnome who pulled pranks until he was fooled by his friends into swearing never to prank again. The rooms downstairs were quiet except for the sounds of the axe hacking through the wooden wall. The children gathered around her, soothed by her song.

Downstairs, the axe hits stopped. Boards creaked, and furniture shifted in the pile. Marcy continued to sing, careful to keep her voice low. The sound of metal hitting metal was followed by grunts and cries of pain. The intruders were at the ambush. "He rued the day he tried to play a prank on Sawson Murrey." There was a roar followed by silence, then another crash of wood breaking and tables shifting. The fighting began again, and the children shook, clinging to her tightly. Marcy started a new song, a memory game that required their participation. Careful not to goad them into responding too loudly, she encouraged them to sing along, filling in the gaps of the song. Another crash and there were more raised voices. She kept the children singing until several minutes went by with no sound of fighting. She nodded to one of the other women in the room, who took over leading the song. Marcy slowly disentangled herself from the group. Cautiously, she peeked past the wall near the stairs. She heard grunting and saw four raiders being dragged, one at a time, back through the hole to the street. Once they were all outside, the men propped furniture against the hole to offer some brief protection from the forces outside.

A horn sounded in the distance. Marcy ran to a window and saw figures emerging from houses and alleys all over the village to walk back over the horizon. "They're leaving!" an archer from one of the upstairs rooms cried as he ran downstairs to the others. The room erupted into massive cheers.

Marcy watched the retreating raiders and wondered at their departure. She looked at the men they killed. Between her fire, the four who broke inside and the ones the archers took out, there were over a dozen. Did the other raiders know so many of their own had died? Did they care? Would they return with reinforcements?

She felt the elation from the survivors and wished she could share in it, but something still stuck in her chest and left her uneasy. They weren't out of this, yet. This was only a temporary reprieve. The real battle was yet to come.

FIVE

"WE APPRECIATE YOU COMING ON SUCH SHORT NOTICE," the mayor said. He was a short, balding man of thin build and wore a dress coat buttoned to the silky white ascot tied at his throat. Large brass buttons adorned the flared, cuffed sleeves. A gold trim followed every seam. His shoes were freshly polished, and his coat was the deepest black, with no hint of fading or specks of lint.

"We strive to answer all calls for our help with matters of legal concern," Mirerien answered, allowing herself to be seated beside the mayor and judge presiding over this case. Her friend and trainer, Collin, sat at the back of the room to serve as a witness to the proceedings. Whenever dealing with other municipalities, it was always wise to have a witness to head off potential political complications should disagreements arise. "Why don't you explain the details behind your need for my mediation in this matter?"

"The defendant is charged with attempting to leave town without paying the balance of fees due for various services," the judge answered her question, clearly thinking that simplistic description was sufficient.

Mirerien looked at the man in question. He was a bridge builder for Saar. According to the reports, he came to Mackenvay to help rebuild a bridge damaged by flooding earlier in the year. Both cities were independently operated with their own local governments and laws. Now, the builder wanted to return to Saar, but Mackenvay insisted he stay to repay fines incurred during his stay. Saar demanded the return of their citizen. Threats of violence loomed large on everyone's minds. A quick resolution of the matter was needed to maintain the peace.

"What have you to say in your defense?" she asked the man.

"Your Majesty," he said with respect, "I came to Mackenvay with the promise of a thousand gold if I helped them rebuild their bridge. They told me ten percent of that would be held back for taxes, but the rest would be mine. Once I arrived here, everything changed. I was told I needed a license to work in the city. To purchase the license, I needed to have insurance to cover my work. I was responsible for providing a meal a day for each of my workers, and if they worked past dusk, I was charged a fine. If they didn't work late and I missed a deadline, I was charged another fine. I had to purchase and pay taxes on all the materials for the build. I could not have my own materials and tools brought into the city without first paying a high tariff. Any materials not used at the end of the job were assessed another fee and returned to the original vendor.

"The money I didn't spend for these things was required to be kept in the city's bank. If I did not put it in the bank, I was told it would be taxed as part of my on-hand assets. But to put it in the bank was a daily fee of three silver coins. At the end of the job, I was charged a fee to remove the money from the bank.

Then when I tried to leave town, I was told there was an exit fee I needed to pay to remove money from their town. I complained I wasn't a citizen and should not be subject to an exit fee, so they said they would charge me the tourist fees instead.

"With only a small amount of gold left, I said I would not pay any more fees or fines. I need what little gold I have left to pay for the journey home and to feed my family once I return. We were depending on the money from this job to get us through the winter months. I just want to go home to my family and forget I ever came here."

"Do you have any financial records I may look over?"

The man gathered his papers and handed them to Mirerien. "Mayor," she said, "please provide me with a copy of your tax code system and a list of all fines, fees, and regulations on the books."

With the requested documents in front of her, Mirerien skimmed through their contents. It was mostly a formality. She knew the man told the truth about his experiences, but she needed concrete numbers and facts to back up that knowledge. It didn't take long to see how easy it was to get in too far. Only a mind with a keen understanding of business could even hope to traverse the relative minefield of unexpected expenses and actually come away with any profit. Closing the books, she pushed them away disgustedly. "Tell me, how many times do you tax the same money?"

"Your Highness, with all due respect," stumbled the mayor, "our taxes are the lowest in the region."

"No, they claim to be only ten percent, but after fees and regulations, your taxes are actually closer to seventy percent, possibly higher in certain circumstances. You mislead people to bring them here."

"These are our laws. It is our right to impose whatever fees we deem necessary for the operation of our city."

"The purpose of law is to maintain order. If you wish to tax your people seventy percent, tax them seventy percent, but be honest about it. What you have created here is a complex system designed to confuse and manipulate people to your advantage. It is deceitful and not in the true spirit of the law. You promised this gentleman only ten percent of his payment would be taxed. Only after he invested his time and money into coming here did you make him aware of these other 'fees' he incurred just by being in possession of the money. It is disingenuous to claim ninety percent of the money is his when it is constantly being depleted whether he spends it or not. You hired this man, brought him far from his home to do a job for the good of the city, taxed him to the point he cannot afford to return home, and now you wish to imprison him until he can earn enough to pay back all of your fees. You have created a system of indentured servitude. This is not the purpose of the law. The bridge builder shall be released and returned five hundred gold to pay for his return to Saar." She leveled her gaze at the smiling builder and spoke seriously. "Should you ever willingly choose to return here, knowing what you know now, you will be subject to all their fees and taxes, whatever they may be."

"Yes, Your Highness. Thank you."

She stood and looked back at the mayor and judge. "I strongly suggest a re-examining of your entire legal code. Should you request help in this endeavor, I can send one of Aleria's legal scholars to consult with. Good day."

Not waiting for their reply, she took her exit. Collin took in the faces of the people in the room and followed. "That was impressive," he said once they were a good distance from the courthouse. "The city officials fully expected you to rule in their favor. They were completely taken off guard by your verdict. Do you think they will change their laws as you suggested?"

"I do not know. As things stand, their allegiance is not to the law but to what manipulations they can achieve through the law. It is possible, once word of the verdict spreads, the citizens here could put sufficient pressure on them to make those changes. Ultimately that decision remains theirs."

"It's amazing how easily you read situations. No matter how hard people try to confuse you or manipulate the facts, you see right through them. You cut straight to the truth."

Mirerien shrugged uncomfortably. Collin had known her since they were very young, but as children, he spent more time with her brothers. She was always around. They were triplets, always close to one another, even when they argued. But Mirerien was aloof, a loner for the most part. Never one to indulge in emotional displays, she preferred calm facts and reason.

Her brother, Pielere, was the one to suggest she begin training with Collin. He was a weapons' master and excellent teacher. Under his tutelage, her skill with the bow and battle hammer had progressed to great heights. Undeterred by her coldness, he worked with her, warming her heart and making her think of things like companionship and family for the first time. But there were things about her he did not know, things he was beginning to notice on his own, like her ability to always know the truth. Somehow, she could sense if a person lied to her. It was a definitive, unquestionable knowledge she could not explain.

Her brothers were gifted with their own unique powers. Pielere could hear the thoughts of their citizens who were in need of justice. Eirae had an ability to evoke a hallucinatory response in criminals to draw out their remorse for wrong done. Their abilities grew stronger with each passing month and seemed to be tied to their roles within the kingdom. Completely dedicated to the law and known as the Three Lawgivers by the people, they were called the Protector, the Punisher, and the Keeper of Order. All of them felt a power behind those names and felt a pull toward their specific calling. It was something they accepted without question, but they struggled with how much to reveal to those close to them.

Mirerien came to a stop at the top of a small hill at the edge of the city and turned to Collin, taking his hands in her own. "About the proposal," she began.

"I know how great your responsibilities are," he interrupted. "I know how many people depend on you and would never do anything to interfere with your duty to them.

"There are things about me you do not know, things I don't even understand," she tried to explain.

"Then let us figure them out together. Whatever may happen, I know my feelings for you. That isn't going to change."

"Collin."

"Oh, Seer of Truth," he said with a smile, not realizing the importance or accuracy of the nickname, "tell me if I lie."

She looked at his smiling face full of love for her and knew he meant those words with his entire being. He beamed with an aura of truth that warmed her with its intensity. And she knew her answer. "I will marry you," she answered. His eyes sparked with excitement, and he spun her in a circle, kissing her deeply.

Staying on the hill, reluctant to rejoin the rest of the world, they watched the sun set and counted stars long into the night until at last one of her attendants called up the hill after them. Sharing one last moment alone, Mirerien bid the woman to approach them.

"Your Majesty, I am sorry to interrupt, but King Pielere sent a message for you."

"Go on," she prompted, listening distractedly.

"He said you were needed back in Aleria right away. He sent a mage to teleport you home. He also said to tell you 'Congratulations.'" The woman looked slightly confused but passed on the message nonetheless.

Mirerien grinned and dismissed the woman. Leave it to Pielere to already know about her engagement. "Well, time to go."

"You don't think that message was about us, do you?" Collin asked.

Mirerien actually laughed, feeling happier than she had in years. "My dear Collin," she said, placing a hand on his cheek. "There are many things you need to know, but that must wait. Let us go home."

———

KERN LOOKED at the expectant faces around him and took a breath. They all sat quietly while he spoke to Thomas through their shared communication rings. Now, they wanted a report. "There has been another raid, north of the border this time."

"In Tynerock?" Lynnalin asked. Kern nodded. "Marcy?"

"Is unharmed," he assured her. "She and Thomas held off the raiders with some of the villagers at the tavern. The rest of the village was not so lucky. They are leading the survivors to the Eastern Ridge."

"That may not be such a bad idea," Zanden said. The main topic of discussion the past few hours had been what to do with the survivors. None of them wanted to drop off a group of women and children somewhere dangerous. Not knowing where the raiders were, where they were going or their numbers, it was impossible to say where may be safe. And travelling any distance with such a group would be slow and difficult. They did not have supplies enough for an extended journey.

The Eastern Ridge, a group of mountains that ran from the coast, all the way up to just east of Aleria and Suriax and farther north, could prove the best option. If they could make it to the caves, they would have cover, possibly enough to hold out for reinforcements. But the ridge was not without its dangers. To get to the protective cover of the caves, one must pass through thick, bramble-filled forests, rough terrain, the howling foothills known for strong, cold winds coming off the mountains and the occasional rockslide. It was not an ideal place to lead a group of ill-dressed women and children, but it was their best option.

The scenery for most of the first day was pleasant, and Kern found himself fall into an almost meditative state of awareness. Grass and acorns crunched underfoot. There were no walking trails here. The trees were thick, growing denser with each hour they walked. Kern stepped over a large fallen tree and reached back, lifting the children one at a time over the obstacle.

They were tired, quiet. Hearing moving water, he called a stop and went to refill the canteens, forage some food and hunt some small game. While their little band of refugees recovered their strength, Kern sat by Lynnalin in the shade of a hill and took a hand full of berries. His stomach growled for something more substantial, but the children needed the energy and nutrition from the meat more than he did. "So, part of a Cinder Unit on assignment for the queen. How did that happen?"

"Just lucky, I guess," Lynnalin answered, taking her own share of the berries.

"Seriously?" he asked

"Seriously? The fire hit, and everything changed. I was at the stadium, watching the tournament like everyone else. I used my magic to help where I could. Apparently, I made a good impression on people."

Kern could believe that. She exuded confidence and strength. The way she followed her ears to the survivors in Breakeren was evidence of that. He had yet to see her fight, though. A lot could be learned about a person by seeing him or her in battle. He wondered, if it came to a fight, how she would fare. But then, she was Suriaxian. Perhaps he should not be so worried.

The wind shifted, and Kern caught the faint smell of smoke. Kern climbed up the hill to their right and jumped up, catching hold of a low hanging branch, using it to swing higher in the tree growing there. Dark plumes of smoke billowed over the hills. The rolling terrain made distance difficult to gauge, but it was close enough to pose a threat. Kern jumped down and dusted off his hands, looking at Lynnalin and Zanden, who had joined them.

"What did you see?" Zanden asked.

"There is possible trouble up ahead. I saw a fire, maybe a few miles north."

Zanden waved the others over. "Rand, Casther, and Lynnalin, I want you to lead the group to the mountains. Kern, you and I will go investigate the source of the fire."

Taking two hounds, they traveled as quickly as possible, only slowing as they came close to their destination and began to hear the screams. Creeping over a low hill, Kern saw his fears realized. A small settlement, nested in the crook of the mountain lay decimated, bodies tossed everywhere, blood, ash, and rubble covering the ground. Monsters wearing scars, and weapons shoved into tortured, mutilated flesh, hacked defenseless farmers and women. One busted a small shed with his fist.

The rickety structure collapsed under the single blow. Children screamed, running from the remains of the structure. A woman pulled herself from the rubble and ran after the children, putting herself between them and their attacker. A piece of wood from the broken wall was her only weapon, but she wielded it with all her strength raising it to block a blow by his battle axe. The axe splintered the wood and dug into her arm. Flinching in pain but not saying a word, she took the broken wood and stabbed at the man.

Kern slid down the hill and ran toward the woman. If only it were that easy. He watched with one eye as she took hit after hit, refusing to back down or abandon the children who cowered behind her. With the other eye, Kern watched for his own safety, fending blows from every raider in his path. He struck out in all directions, cutting tendons and opening arteries to bleed out. There was no time to personally dispatch each opponent. The woman dropped to one knee, her other leg broken by a rebounding blow from the back of the axe. A child cried behind her. The man's attention shifted. The woman saw his axe lift and aim at the child, a small girl no older than five. With nothing left to do, she threw herself on the girl, determined to take the hit herself.

Just as it came within inches of her head, the axe stopped, held in place by the force of Kern's sword. Kern pushed on the axe, throwing the man temporarily off balance. Pressing his advantage, Kern followed through, stabbing his chest and piercing his heart with a single blow. The man staggered back, still in shock at the unexpected resistance and turn of events. He tried to strike again, but his body was already dead. As his brain finally ran out of blood, his eyes closed, and his body fell lifeless to the ground.

There was no time to celebrate, though. Five more men came up in his place, and they would not be taken by surprise.

AMANDA YOUNG & RAYMOND YOUNG JR.

He heard the children crying. The woman said words of reas-
surance, quieting their fears and pulling them to her. Her body
was all but useless. Still, she used it as a shield. Determined not
to allow her sacrifices to be in vain, Kern took a centering
breath and launched his attack. He hit their weapon arms first,
severing the ones he could, disabling all the rest. Blows that
would have crippled other warriors caused barely a flinch.
Where one arm was gone, they used the other. Kern took a
heavy punch to the jaw, followed by a hit in the gut that left
him winded. But if they could press on, so could he.

Taking advantage of his doubled over posture, Kern
rammed the man closest to him. He didn't expect to move him
far, but he did not need to. Once in close, he shoved his short
sword up under the man's ribs, going in from the gut. Pulling
the blade out at an angle, he stepped back, twisting out of the
way of another attacker. He used his smaller size to slip under
the man's reach and strike up with his blade. The sword went
in just below the chin and pierced all the way through the
brain. He pulled the sword and sent it straight behind him, into
the belly of the next man. Unlike the other two blows, this was
not enough to instantly kill the man. He brought his arm down
hard on Kern's shoulder, but that was not the worst of it. The
man's arm was covered in a series of metal shards, standing out
like claws or horns on an animal. The shards ripped into his
shoulder and neck. Kern took a step to the side, but the man hit
again, leaving a trail of gashes down his arm.

Time slowed in that moment. Gathering his center again,
he heard the children crying. The woman was silent. Her body
was still. He didn't have long if he hoped to save her. It may
already be too late. Across the yard, Zanden fought off four
large brutes. Blue fire slid down his blade, covering his fists and
burning his adversaries. Despite that advantage, the numbers
they faced were high. Like Kern, Zanden had taken his fair

share of abuse. Kern took another punch to the gut and thought absentmindedly that he ought to worry about saving himself. Pushing that thought to the side, Kern pressed on. They may be fighting monsters, and he did not have the benefit of Suriaxian fire, but that did not mean he would give up. The next time the man swung Kern moved with him, using his momentum to carry the man into one of the other two remaining opponents. The two men began fighting each other, leaving Kern with the last man.

Kern ducked and stabbed, sticking holes into the man wherever possible. Not that the pain would stop him, but he hoped in the absence of a killing blow, blood loss could eventually win out. Too bad Kern was fighting his own share of blood loss. He aimed for the sensitive areas of the wrists and ankles, but the man's skin was tough and difficult to cut through effectively. Kern dropped and rolled out of the man's reach, picking up a discarded axe along the way. Giving it a throw, he was rewarded by a solid stick in the man's forehead. He fell instantly.

From the two men who had forgotten Kern to start their own brawl, a single victor stood. It was the same clawed-arm man who caused Kern so much pain before. Not giving the man a chance to attack again Kern swung low, cutting off one leg entirely and the other leg in half. Unable to stand, the man fell to his back. Kern stabbed down, intending to end it all with a clean hit to the heart. Unfortunately, unable to stand did not mean unable to fight. That clawed arm struck out and pulled Kern off his own feet. Kern hit the ground hard. Still struggling to pull air back into his lungs, he stabbed up under the man's arm. Sharp metal tore into Kern's forearm with every movement. Kern ignored the pain and pushed the sword in deeper, twisting it until the man stopped moving.

With a deep breath in, Kern crawled over to the woman

and children. The children were afraid but alive. Kern lifted the woman off the children she shielded, even while unconscious. Her chest moved faintly with shallow breaths. He pulled a potion from his bag and poured it down her throat. She coughed but did not rouse. Her wounds were deep. She lived, but barely. It could take a dozen potions to heal her damage. Kern looked around the battlefield. People lay dead and dying. Zanden, having dispatched the other Cullers, now walked around handing out potions and doing field dressings.

Kern tried another potion on the woman, but like the first, it did very little to help her. He looked at the hopeful faces of the children she gave everything to save and pulled off his cloak, wrapping it around her broken body. Picking her up, he ignored the bruised and torn muscles of his arms and carried her. The children followed close behind. "Come with us."

"Look over there," one of the townspeople called from the top of the hill.

Kern took one look at the man's face and climbed up to him to see what had him so afraid. Past the treetops, and the foothills, at the base of the valley, sat a camp, a very large camp. They were too far away to make out many details, but from the number of fires and tents he saw, they were looking at a group of substantial proportions. "Let's go," he said, staring at the plumes of smoke and feeling a rise of terror run through him. "Let's go."

———

"What should we do?"

Traxton heard the mix of uncertainty and excitement in his friend's question. Bricksben shifted, silent despite the dead grass and leaves at their feet. Martiene crouched beside him, equally quiet and just as excited. His eyes beamed. There were both practically salivating at the prospects of the battle ahead. On the other side of the tree line stood the thing the three of them had spent months searching for. They found the Culler camp.

But it was much larger than they expected. Cullers normally travelled alone or in small bands, quickly reduced by infighting or by people going off on their own. They abhorred order and rules. They thrived on chaos. Cullers were a force that could not be controlled or contained, only temporarily directed. They could never be completely destroyed. Even if every one of them was eradicated today, another would arise tomorrow. They were creatures of instinct, fed by bloodlust, crazed by snippets of knowledge and insights mortals were never meant to have and subjects of a god most of their kind did not know the name of. They worshiped him, not with prayers or rituals but with death and destruction. Their actions spread his teachings, infecting other susceptible minds with its corrupt meanings. They were pawns, used and thrown away as needed.

Yet, there were hundreds, maybe thousands of them here. They were traveling, living, and fighting together, if reports of earlier raids were to be believed. And indeed, their own research supported those reports. Smaller groups did split off to plunder the random village, but they then rejoined the whole. It was unprecedented and reason for pause. Going down there to face this horde would be suicide. While some armies may be tricked or demoralized by the magic clones their three-man group often used to make their numbers appear greater, as they had with that gathering of warriors burning bodies at Breakeren, such ploys would not make a difference here. Traxton did not fear death, but to die for no reason, while their enemy survived, was pointless. They needed to learn more and develop a strategy of attack to wipe out as many of the enemy as possible.

"We wait." He felt their eyes turn on him in surprise and disappointment. Their hatred of the Cullers ran deep, all the way to their gods. The Sublinates followed Randik, a god of war and battle. According to his teachings, conflict was inevitable, but through battle, skilled warriors could tap into the art of sublime combat

Raze gloried in destruction. It was not enough to defeat an opponent in open combat. You must tear their body to shreds, pummel their flesh and spirit, terrorize and break their minds, destroy their homes and families and wipe them completely out of existence. His followers carried these teachings into their treatment of their own bodies. Unlike Sublinates who used magic and training to meld with weapons to become a weapon, Cullers would rip and destroy their own flesh, forcing it to accept the weapons they shoved in their bodies. Instead of designing blades to grow with their bones, they replaced their bones with blades. They were completely out of harmony within themselves and the world.

It was argued by the early Cullers, before they lost their minds to the chaos, that destruction was also a natural component of war. While the Sublinates agreed with that sentiment, they also believed it was not an aspect of war to revel in. War was inevitable. Destruction was inevitable. There would always be conflicts and death. Wars served a purpose, to unite nations behind a cause, free people from oppression and settle disagreements. They were a natural process that allowed life to grow and develop. From the ashes new hope, governments and opportunities could form. By focusing completely on the destruction, they ignored the good and shamefully turned their attacks on noncombatants. It was dishonorable.

The Great War of Wars between Sublinates and Cullers raged on a good three decades and killed nearly everyone involved. Countries evacuated to make room for their battles.

Those who felt the call of Raze or Randik traveled across continents to join in the conflict. Finally, lone survivors of various battles moved on, unaware who lived elsewhere. Thought extinct, they faded into the history scrolls, thus relegated to myths. The Sublinates now welcomed the anonymity. Traveling in secrecy, they tracked down reports of extreme cruelness and violence to put down newly awakened Cullers before their madness could spread. It was an endless, thankless task, but it was necessary.

"We can't wait," Bricksben argued. "They are camped. We are away from any large towns. If we wait, they will continue to raid and grow even stronger."

"We need to learn more about this moving camp of theirs," Traxton cautioned. "They are organized. We are vastly outnumbered. We must determine their weakness before we act."

"Info, got it," Martiene said, bounding up from his position and slipping through the trees. He was invisible and gone before Traxton could argue. He shook his head. Martiene was one of the few in the world equally skilled in the blade and magic. Not as powerful as a full wizard, he could cast many useful combat spells. His unusual skill set made him impulsive and reckless at times. Whether out of need to prove himself to those better at weapon or hand to hand combat, or from an overabundance of confidence in the ability of his versatile skills to get him out of trouble, he often acted without hesitation or a plan.

Traxton nodded at Bricksben and motioned left. He took right. Moving silently, they circled the camp, taking position should Martiene need assistance.

MARTIENE SYSTEMATICALLY WORKED his way to the large tent at the center of the camp. It sat clustered in an area of other tents, but this one clearly stood out for its size and the clean, orderly condition of the surrounding area. The inside of the tent was quiet and still. Heavy fabric blocked many of the sounds from outside. Curtains offset three rooms within the tent.

The first was mostly empty, a large receiving room with a wooden bench on the far side and not much else of note. Curtains on either side of the bench led to the other two rooms, including one that served as a bedroom. The cot, nearly ten feet in length, took up most of the space. Beside it was a small table and lantern.

Pushing past the curtain to the other room, he found an open chest of maps and notes. Sorting through them he found cities scratched out all across the plains, down to the coast. There were even a few marks around the cliffs. As far as Martiene could tell, each mark indicated a place destroyed by Cullers. There were a lot of marks.

Flipping through the papers, he found another set of maps highlighting areas further north. The marks on these maps seemed to indicate areas well known for skilled or powerful fighters. Checking the other maps, he saw many corresponding marks along the path they took. There was only one explanation he could reason for what he saw. They were recruiting new Cullers. Otherwise, why would they travel directly through areas they knew would have the strongest opposition? Cullers loved a good fight, but this group was organized and obviously traveling with a destination in mind. By travelling this path, they weeded out weaker members and took on new people, thereby ensuring their army would continue to strengthen and grow as it moved. It was brilliant, but where were they going? What was the purpose behind everything?

Without warning, a blade pressed in at his throat. Martiene threw back his arm reflexively and hit the person holding the blade. She went tumbling through the curtain doorway, back into the entrance room. Pushing his way through the outside wall, Martiene ran, his caution and stealth lost in the urgency of the moment. He could hear the woman follow him through the camp. Others soon became aware of his presence and followed suit. Still clutching the maps, he pulled his hands together in a series of hand signals and cast his clone spell. Exact replicas ran off in each direction, confusing some of those pursuing him. Fighting his way to the edge of the camp, he saw Bricksben adding cover for his escape. He raised a hand in thanks only to see Bricksben fall mid-bow pull by a spear to the chest. He could not see Traxton, but from the sound of battle on the opposite side of camp, he could wager a bet he was over there, too far to be of any immediate help.

Martiene stopped running and dropped the maps, pulling his sword. He wouldn't live long enough to show the maps to anyone anyway. He might as well go out fighting. Feeling more thrilled than he should at the prospect of his final battle, Martiene struck with deadly precision, glorying in each kill.

Then a shadow fell upon the battlefield. Martiene turned and faced a wall of flesh and muscle. A massive fist slammed into his chest, breaking three ribs on contact and sending him flying across the camp. He groaned and tried to move. The bones pressing into his lungs made that difficult. The end of a staff pushed against his broken bones and made breathing all but impossible.

"Wait," a woman called.

Martiene cracked open his eyes and watched a young girl approach. No, he amended, not a girl but a halfling woman. A nice-sized bruise blossomed on the side of her face, and he recognized her as the person from the tent. "Ah, so you want to be the one to kill me," he said, his voice raw and cracking.

"No," she said, crossing her legs and sitting in front of him. "I have something special in mind for you." Casually she put a hand on his leg. Her hair shifted from blonde to bright green. Then everything went dark.

SIX

THE SURVIVORS OF EVEREND, THE POOR, DESTROYED
village in the foothills of the Eastern Ridge, were actually a
great help in bypassing many of the dangers on the way to the
mountains. They knew the passageways safe from the wind
and the paths with easier footing for a group of injured. The
women from Breakeren were quick to help care for their
injuries. Unable to help their own families survive those
monsters, they were eager to ease the pain of these new
survivors. The children, being children, played.

They traveled until nightfall made travel too dangerous and
set up camp in the shadow of the mountains. The next day
would find them safely in its caves. Kern helped the survivors
get settled, making sure everyone had food and water, and
made his way over to the woman in his cloak. She woke up an
hour or so into the journey, but her recovery was slow. She still
had trouble walking very far, and her breathing was rough.
Kern handed her a canteen of fresh water and a bag of berries.
"I know it isn't much," he apologized.

"It is fine," she assured him. "I'm Samantha, by the way. All the times we've talked since I woke up, and I realized I never told you my name."

He smiled. "I'm Kern."

"Well, Kern, not that I'm complaining, but why did you put this wonderful, much-appreciated healing cloak around me, when you could obviously use it for yourself? And where did you even get such a thing?"

"As to the where, it was a gift from my siblings. And I put it on your because, after the way you defended those children, I thought you deserved to be saved." At first, he thought she fought to defend her own children, but that was not the case. Once things settled down, he saw the children claimed by their own surviving family members. She nearly died protecting other people's children. "The way you took those hits without once crying out in pain was amazing."

"I did not want to frighten the children," she looked down shyly, uncomfortable with the praise. "I just wish this were all some nightmare. I keep thinking I am going to wake up safe in my home."

The forest melted away, replaced by an ornate palace room. Samantha blinked. A woman and two men, all extremely well dressed, stood around a table on the far side of the room. They looked up at her in surprise.

"That is Kern's cloak," the woman said.

One of the men came over to her and grabbed the cloak at her shoulder. She winced from the pain of injuries still unhealed. "Where did you get this?" he demanded.

"A man, a warrior told me to wear it to heal my injuries."

"Some warrior you do not know just gave you a highly magical item?" he asked incredulously.

"My village was attacked. I was badly injured. The stranger protected us, killing many of the raiders and leading us to safety. My village had no magic, potions, healers or clerics. He told me to wear the cloak until I felt better."

The man looked back at the woman, who nodded. He released his hold on her shoulder and stepped back. The other man held out a hand. "I'm Pielere. This is Mirerien and Eirae."

"My Lords," she bowed, immediately recognizing their names.

Pielere smiled warmly and led her over to the table. "Tell us about your village, where it is, anything you remember about the raiders, and where your people are now. But first," he grinned, "tell us your name." His demeanor had the desired effect and put her nerves at ease.

"My name is Samantha."

"It is wonderful to meet you. Let us get a cleric to heal the remainder of Samantha's injuries," he said to the two guards she had not noticed stood at the chamber door. "And find her some new clothing."

The guards bowed and left. Samantha proceeded to fill the monarchs in on all that happened, careful not to leave out any details they may find useful. When she finished, the queen led her to a room, even more lavish than the last. Samantha felt self-conscious, even standing on the pristine, plush rugs that covered the floor. Her shoes and clothes were covered in dirt and dried blood. Her dress was in tatters. She pulled the cloak tighter. Two women followed them to the chamber. One held an assortment of gowns. The other carried potions and scrolls.

"Hand me the cloak," Mirerien instructed.

Samantha reluctantly complied. The cleric gasped. "My word, where did you receive such gashes? How long did you wear the cloak?" She began prodding the wounds. Samantha winced reflexively.

"Since shortly after mid-day," Samantha answered the

second question, not in the mood to relive her report to the three Alerian lords.

"And the injuries are still so deep? You are lucky to be alive and still in possession of all your limbs. It is a wonder you did not lose this arm." She indicated a particularly bad gash on her right arm.

"Can you help her?" Mirerien asked, handing the cloak to the other attendant to clean.

"Yes, Your Majesty, but it will take some time."

Mirerien nodded. "Lorise will see to your needs once Setta finishes healing your injuries."

"Thank you, Your Majesty."

———

MIRERIEN SIGHED HEAVILY and put the place marker back down on the map. She and her brothers spent the entire night pouring over reports and discussing strategy. To send troops without leaving the city vulnerable to attack was no easy business. If they sent too few troops, they could doom the mission before it began. Without knowing how many they faced or what drove these raiders, it was impossible to guess their next move.

The light of the rising sun streamed in from the window, falling on Kern's cloak, folded neatly on the dais. The cloak faded into the light, disappearing before their eyes. Moments later, Kern appeared, wearing it.

Mirerien felt a rush of relief. After seeing the extent of the girl's injuries, she worried how badly Kern may have been hurt, but he looked to be in relatively good shape. He smiled at seeing them and gave them each a welcoming hug. She could tell from the way Pielere and Eirae's shoulders and faces relaxed that they shared her concerns and relief.

"You know," Pielere chastised, "when we gave you the cloak, it was not so you could give it to the first pretty girl you saw."

"I know, I know," Kern said, looking appropriately chagrined. "I didn't think she would make it. Two healing potions barely did anything, and there were many other people with severe injuries who needed the few remaining potions I had."

"And what of your injuries?" Eirae turned Kern's arm to show the many cuts and bruises slowly beginning to heal under the cloak's magic.

"I've had worse." He shrugged. "Besides, we have more important things to worry about right now."

"The raiders," Pielere agreed.

"Not just raiders, Cullers."

No one spoke for several seconds. "Are you sure?" Mirerien asked, already knowing the answer. She could feel the truth and certainty in his words.

Kern nodded and told them everything he saw, from the bodies and Sublinates in Breakeren to his battle in Everend.

"I always thought the Cullers were a legend, a myth," Mirerien said, mostly to herself.

"I was afraid of this," Pielere said, catching them all off guard. "I've had dreams," he explained. "Ever since they crossed the border, I woke up hearing screams. I dream through the eyes of those tortured and killed by terrifying, mutilated monsters. I thought ... I hoped they were simply nightmares. I knew it was not. That was the real reason I asked you back early from your trip," he confessed to Mirerien.

"How many would you say there are?" Eirae asked Kern.

"There were easily a thousand in the camp I saw. The group that attacked Tynerock had several hundred. A dozen or more attacked at Everend. There's no way to know how many other smaller groups may be separated from the main one."

"We may not have enough troops to send, not while keeping enough to protect Aleria from an impromptu Suriaxian attack. Maerishka will likely take any reduction in our forces as an open invitation to invade." Pielere sat heavily.

"She would likely claim our forces were being sent to attack her in the Southern Plains," Eirae agreed.

"Why not talk to her?" Kern suggested. "They attacked her lands and people as well as yours. This threat is bigger than family rivalry. We could work together."

All three monarchs scoffed. "We could never trust her not to betray us in the midst of battle," said Mirerien.

Pielere and Eirae nodded their agreement. Kern paused, clearly wanting to argue the point, but decided against it. "Whatever you do, I need to get supplies and get back to the survivors."

"You can't go alone," Mirerien argued.

"I can't stay here. I'm needed there. Those people are afraid. Many are hurt. I won't abandon them."

"About Maerishka," Pielere started.

Kern held up a hand." That's all diplomacy and politics, and frankly, I don't want any part of it. You guys do what you need to do. I will do what I need to do."

"Just don't get yourself killed," Eirae said with a smile.

Kern smiled back. "I'll do my best."

Mirerien hugged her brother and couldn't help the severe sense of foreboding that overtook her. "Make sure you do."

Kern drew back, his face serious once more as he searched her eyes for the meaning behind her tone. "I will," he swore. And then he left.

It DIDN'T TAKE LONG for word of his return to spread. Kern handed out what potions he had, keeping a few hidden for later, and passed out rations to the hungry survivors. He gave shoes and coats to those without. The caves would be colder than outside, and they still had to travel over patches of sharp rocks in the mouth of the cave to access the deeper tunnels. He handed out the last coat and thanked the gods he had enough for everyone who needed one. It cost all the gold in his pouch, but he would do it again.

"You are back," Zanden said. "What did you learn?"

"Not much." Kern followed him off to the side. Casther and Rand sat cleaning and sharpening their weapons. Lynnalin was nowhere around. "Aleria may send some troops, but they don't know how many or when." He sat heavily on a tree stump. "They are concerned Suriax may choose to attack while their defenses are down."

Rand made a noise in his throat. "She probably would, too. I was surprised she didn't push matters after the Night of Blue Fire."

Casther shook his head. "It wouldn't have been a strategic move to launch an attack before we learned to control the fire and fight with it. We would have been just as likely to kill our own men. Now, however ..."

The air shifted, and Lynnalin appeared before them. She took one look at their faces and sighed. "I take it your visit was as productive as mine," she said to Kern.

"Where did you go?"

"Suriax."

"Are they sending reinforcements?" Zanden asked hopefully.

"A few, but nothing substantial. She doesn't want to move an army through Alerian lands. She said she would post some sentries at the border to keep the raiders from returning, but now that they are in Alerian territory, they are Aleria's problem."

"She holds back our troops, knowing Aleria will likely need to send theirs," Rand said. "Sounds like it is to be war between us, after all." They all fell quiet in their thoughts.

Those thoughts were interrupted as a small girl, no older than three, ran up to Kern and hugged his leg. "Thank you for the food and shoes," she said, giving his leg a kiss. The child's mother ran up and picked up the girl.

"I am sorry for the intrusion," she said. "Marie just really wanted to thank you. So did I." The woman smiled gratefully and carried the child away. She peeked over her mother's shoulder as they left. Kern felt himself smile despite the severity of their situation. It didn't matter if they were Suriaxian or Alerian. He knew he would do whatever it took to protect these people.

———

MOST OF THE blood was dry, except a few gooey red puddles of mud formed by spilled water from an overturned trough. The smell of death and burnt flesh filled the air. Surprisingly, a large number of the dead belonged to their army. Their people were restless and ruthless, often striking out on their own to relieve their urges. Most returned to the group within a few days. In all the places they stopped to raid on their northward journey across the continent, they only ever lost a few here or there, always much fewer than they killed, and they never left survivors other than for recruiting purposes. But now the game had changed. First came reports from that small border town about the woman with the blue fire. Now an even smaller settlement showed signs of survivors' tracks and Cullers killed by fire. Something strange was going on. How exciting!

Following the tracks, Ridikquelass found herself at the opening of a large cave. Unused branches sat on ash and kindling in several evenly spaced piles outside the cave. They came here, and from the quantity of used up fire pits she saw, there was a significant number in their group. She knelt and touched one of the branches. It was cool, but she could still feel a little heat from the ashes underneath. Going a short ways into the cave, she looked for signs of dirt disturbed on the floor and found all the tracks led to a tunnel heading north.

Somewhere in the mountains traveled someone, possibly the blue fire witch, strong enough to fight back and survive a Culler attack. If they could find this person and capture her, they could possibly convert her into one of them, or at least learn where she got her power. At the very least, they could kill her.

Ridikquelass ran quickly back to the camp. Her three bushy ponytails bobbed the entire way. The journey through the mountains would be slow and tiresome, especially given the size of the group she suspected was in there. But she had a good idea where they were going. There was only one place large enough to give them any hope of safety. Traveling closer to established routes, skirting the foothills and rougher terrain, her group should be able to catch up and cut them off from reinforcements. Grabbing the horn, she handed it to Nadda, filling her in. Nadda nodded, her conch shell pendant swinging forward with the movements. She raised the horn to her lips, waiting for Ridikquelass to cover her ears, and blew. A loud blast sounded through the camp, echoing for miles, reverberating off metal and breaking glass. Without another word or command, the Cullers grabbed their things, packed up the camp, and started moving. Now, the real fun would begin.

SEVEN

THE AIR WAS COOL AND HUMID. WATER DRIPPED DOWN from the ceiling. It was a constant sound in the darkness and an occasional slipping hazard. Balls of magic light floated around them, but they did not penetrate far into the shadows. Progress was slow. The stone floor was slick in spots, making caution and careful steps a necessity. Not that anyone had the energy to walk with speed. Hours of travelling through these dark caves had taken its toll. Everyone was anxious to feel the warmth of the sun. The only one who did not seem to mind the journey was Rand. Through the haze of the lantern light, Kern could almost swear he saw the dwarf skip a couple of times. He knew he heard the man humming softly. After years of living and growing up in the openness and trees of Suriax, being in these caves was like coming home.

If his jovial attitude annoyed anyone, they had the good sense not to say anything. They were lucky to have him here, and everyone knew it. Without Rand's unfailing sense of direction, they could easily become lost or turned around down here. The caves twisted and turned, branching into dead ends and bottomless drop-offs. Underground rivers, fed by runoff from the Therion River, ran throughout. Several times they were forced to double back and try alternate paths. Rand kept them traveling north, to safety.

"How are the short legs doing?" Zanden asked, joining Kern at the back.

Kern grinned. 'Short legs' was their nickname for the youngest walking children. They were stubborn enough to insist on walking, heavy enough that their mothers didn't put up much of an argument, and young enough to become easily distracted by random rocks and dark tunnels. "They are tired but holding up. No complaining, but they are starting to fall behind."

Zanden nodded. "We should stop for a while, get something to eat, and let the children get some rest. We can get started again in the morning, or afternoon, or whatever time of day it is outside these blasted caves."

Kern chuckled. Their elven natures were prickling in these confines. In many ways, the humans they led were doing better than their protectors. They were certainly complaining less.

They set up camp and let everyone rest, taking turns on watches. The passage of time was impossible to track. Kern watched the light from the lantern spell flicker and cast shadows on the wall. After what felt like an hour, but could have been more or less, he began to fall into a light, far from restful sleep. Footsteps echoed softly down the tunnels, perking his elven ears. He opened his eyes and listened, unsure at first if he dreamt the sounds. No, they were real, if far away. Someone or something was in the caves.

Kern made his way quietly to the outside edges of the group and knelt by Casther, who acknowledged his presence with a distracted nod. Most of his attention was focused on the direction of the sounds. "What can you hear?" Kern asked.

"Just the footsteps, now, but I heard voices a short while ago. From the sound of things, I'd say there are a lot of them."

"Do you think it's the raiders?" Kern asked softly, not wanting to frighten anyone who might be awake.

Casther shook his head. "The footsteps are slow, shuffled, tired. I doubt that is them."

"The refugees from Tynerock?" Kern asked

He nodded. "That would be my guess. You should take Rand and check it. I will wake Zanden and Lynn."

Kern did as he was asked and woke Rand. He acknowledged Kern with a grunt and rolled off his mat, ready to go. Without Lynnalin's lantern light spell, the caves were impossibly dark. Rand suggested traveling without a light in case Casther was wrong about the identity behind the sounds. They walked perhaps fifty feet when Kern gave up and asked to light a torch. His toes were aching from stubbing them on rocks and his grunts of discomfort and surprise every time he walked into a wall or low ledge gave away any hint of surprise they might have. Besides, the darkness was not helping his feelings of claustrophobia. He wanted a light.

Rand laughed and pulled out his hammer, wrapping it in blue Suriaxian fire. The caves were even more unsettling cast in the blue hue, but he could finally see and avoid the rocks, so Kern counted his blessings and tried not to think about his anxiety. As the sounds grew louder, it became easier.

"I told you we already went this way," a man's voice said. "There is the mark I left on the wall." Several voices broke out into argument about which way to go, which way they already went and how long they would be trapped in these caves. Dim yellow light shone around the corner up ahead. Rand extinguished his fire, and they walked confidently the last few dozen feet to their destination. Marcy was the first to notice them, her elven ears giving her the advantage in hearing their approach over the uproar of the tired, angry and frightened survivors of Tynerock.

"Kern!" she called excitedly, rushing over. "I am so glad to see you." She collided into him and wrapped him in a warm hug.

Thomas walked over with a similar grin. Most of the others settled down, distracted and curious by the unexpected interruption. "Please tell me you know a way out of here. We've been traveling in circles for what feels like months."

"Only one month," Kern teased.

"Actually," Rand corrected them both, "it's only been about five days."

"Only." Kern rolled his eyes. "You guys stay here for now. Get some rest while you can. We'll get everyone else and continue on in the morning, night, whatever."

———

THE AIR WAS STALE. Samantha held her hand to her chest and tried to calm her pounding heart. Once that was under control, she trained all her senses to determine what woke her. All was quiet. She felt the insistent pressure on her chest and rose, letting the sheets fall to the ground. Her bare feet padded determinedly to the window. She looked out into the darkness. A few random lanterns lit the two cities, but most people were asleep at this hour. Her stomach turned. She lowered her head. Taking a brief moment to reassure herself she wasn't imagining things, Samantha rushed from her chamber.

She ignored the looks from the guards and waited with as much patience as she could gather. It did not take long to gain admittance to the room she first arrived at. As she guessed, the monarchs were still wide awake. She could see the fatigue on their faces, but they still mustered friendly smiles in greeting.

"What can we do for you?" Pielere asked.

Samantha gathered a burst of courage and spoke. "I believe we are in imminent danger." Pielere raised an eyebrow but motioned for her to continue. "Just before my people were attacked, I felt this overwhelming sickness. I ignored it then," she admitted, to her shame. "Within minutes, they were upon us. I just awoke with the same feeling. A great evil approaches."

The three shared a look. "What do you hear?" Mirerien asked Pielere.

He closed his eyes. The room fell quiet. "Fear. In the outer farming settlements."

"Those were evacuated," Eirae argued.

"Someone must have stayed," Mirerien reasoned.

Eirae cursed under his breath. "If we send our fastest unit ..."

Pielere sucked in a sharp breath and shook his head. "Too late." Eirae cursed again.

"Where did you feel the call?" Mirerien asked.

Pielere studied the map for a moment and pointed to a spot roughly a day's walk from the Suriaxian wall, at the south of their two cities. Mirerien pointed to a spot parallel on the map, in the mountains. "That is where I sense Kern."

"So, the raiders are tracking the refugees," Eirae surmised.

"Either that," Pielere said, "or it is a very bad coincidence."

Mirerien pointed to a spot in the mountains slightly north. "This is where they will likely exit the caves." The tunnels north of that point curved away from the cities. That point bent the closest to Suriax and Aleria.

"That's almost two thousand yards from even Suriax's walls. They'll be slaughtered, in the open like that, long before they can make it to the cities." Eirae stepped back in frustration.

"What can I do?" Samantha asked, unable to remain quiet any longer.

"Can you fight?" Eirae asked.

Samantha looked away in shame. "I can lift a sword, but I possess very little skill in wielding one. I was just an assistant farrier. I'm afraid I don't have many useful skills."

Pielere walked up and put a hand on her shoulder. "I wouldn't say that. This feeling you had, other than the previous attack, have you felt it before?"

Samantha thought back. "Once. A stranger came through our settlement. He needed his horse re-shoed. Every time he came near, I felt ill. He was friendly. Everyone liked him well enough. He did not hurt anyone or start any fights. After he left, the feeling went away. A week later, soldiers came looking for him. He was an escaped criminal, wanted for murder."

Pielere nodded, satisfied by her answer. "I want you to stay in these chambers. There is a door over there," he inclined his head to the far wall. "Push in the knob to the left, and it will open. Our families will be in the adjoining rooms. If you get that feeling again, strong enough to convince you the palace is no longer safe, lead them through that door."

Her eyes widened at the enormity of the task she was given. He was placing the lives of his children in her hands. "Yes, Sir," was all she could say. He gave her that comforting smile again, and she felt much of her fear melt away. With a nod, the three of them left as one, calling out to the attendants and issuing orders before the door even finished closing behind them.

THE ROOM WAS QUIET. Children lined the walls. Their backs were pressed straight. Their posture was perfect. The only thing that betrayed their age was their eyes. In her presence, adults would stare forward or at their feet. These children watched her every move, looking her straight in the eye. They were unafraid of her power. Fed by the illusion of youthful immortality, they indulged their curiosity, completely unintimidated.

Maerishka walked to the next room and knew they were finally at the older students. The girls all wore hair cut short, above the shoulders. For females of elven descent, this was an unusual sight. The boys and girls all wore bright, new clothing. Shoes were perfectly kept with no signs of wear. The many burn scars were finally beginning to heal. These children were hit harder than most by the Night of Blue Fire that gave all adult Suriaxians their gift. They were mostly children, barely past puberty and lacking the discipline needed to quickly control the fire. Even the adults struggled with this. It took over a month to develop their skills to the point where they could return to school without accidentally burning everything to the ground.

To accommodate those early accidents and to help the girls stay alive, most cut their hair right way. When flames erupted in the middle of the night or during play, long hair was a hazard that could quickly catch fire. Even with that precaution, most burned through a great deal of their wardrobe, hence all the new clothing.

Despite their struggles and injuries, they showed no self-pity or signs of trauma. Even standing still and respectful, their excitement filled the room. As with the younger children, many met her gaze head-on. A few smiled. She felt a flush of pride and respect. These students were the future of Suriax. They were strong, and her kingdom would be stronger for them.

When she made her vow to Venerith, she could never have known what would happen. She prayed for his blessings and the strength to maintain her power. She gave him her citizens in the bargain. At first, she lamented sharing his gift of fire with her subjects, but now she saw the wisdom of his choice. With a people this dangerous, outside forces would be fools to challenge her and her kingdom. Should a challenge come from within, as they so often did, her fire still burned hottest. She could burn from over ten feet away and kill with a touch. Her attendants and husband were forced to take potions and drape themselves in protective magic to hazard being near her. It was a good bargain.

Maerishka exchanged a few words with the teachers and headmaster, finalizing details of the rebuilding efforts. There were rooms to imbue with protective spells, scrolls to replace and other less pressing concerns. Maerishka nodded and politely disengaged herself from the discussion. Any other issues could be addressed by her staff. Making her way back to the palace, she looked around the city. There was still a great deal of work to do. Most of the rebuilding was completed. Her people were hard-working and determined. But the scars were there. Empty lots sat where homes and businesses once stood. Char marks shone on doors and pavement. The people smiled and bustled about, but more than a few bore new scars. Some sported fresh burns. They were still adjusting. This would take time.

She turned the corner and hurried to the palace, stopping at the look of excited agitation displayed by the guards. They looked away nervously in her presence. Before she could question them, Svanteese rushed up. "Your Majesty," he said, slightly out of breath.

Svanteese was her most trusted royal advisor and had a way of always being around while rarely being noticed. He heard everything and was a great political asset with extensive knowledge in affairs of state and a quick mind. Svanteese was also a good man, sometimes caring a bit too much for what happened to people he felt were undeserving of punishment. Despite that character flaw, he was a hard worker and a great help in managing affairs of state.

"What is it?" she asked, surprised to see him so out of sorts.

"You have visitors," he answered carefully.

Leaving the guards to their discomfort, she proceeded to follow Svanteese through the foyer toward the visitor sitting room. Curious who could get the palace in such a stir, she didn't bother asking any further questions. Instead, she flung open the double doors and gasped in shock. Pielere, Mirerien, and Eirae stood waiting for her. She felt her palms burn and wished briefly her gloves were gone.

"Hello, Sister." Eirae grinned at her reaction.

"You may go," she said to Svanteese before closing the doors behind her. "I assume there is some reason for this visit."

Pielere rose from his seat next to Mirerien. Eirae remained lounging arrogantly against a chair. "We are here to discuss a matter of importance to both our cities. The raiders from the Southern Plains have continued their northward path. They will be at the wall soon."

Maerishka laughed, her tension gone. "Is that all? Let them come. No one can get through our wall." The outer wall that wrapped around both Suriax and Aleria was a massive construction. Solid stone, it measured thirty feet high and was over ten feet thick, more in some spots. Watchtowers sat at each corner and by all access points. Guards patrolled para-pet-embellished walkways at the top of the wall. An attack from Aleria was a much greater threat than any outward force breaching their defenses. As they were once one city, the walls separating them were much thinner and easier to overcome.

"And what of the survivors from their earlier raids?" Pielere asked. "Even now, they make their way through the mountains.

They will be slaughtered the moment they leave the protection of the caves.

Maerishka narrowed her eyes. "Since you seem to know so much about my people, you should also know the refugees are not unprotected."

"And you think a four-man team is any match against an army of Cullers?" Eirae asked.

Maerishka bristled but refused to comment on their knowledge of the size of her team. Instead, she focused on the latter part of her question. "Yes, I've heard those rumors as well. Don't tell me you actually believe that nonsense. The Cullers were wiped out in the wars."

"The men who lived during those times died. The ideas they fought for, the mindset of chaos, destruction, and rage, are not so easily overcome." Eirae stood and dropped his casual posture. "These raiders travel as a plague, engulfing any place they touch, killing without mercy, standing and continuing to fight with no regards to their own pain or death. Whatever their goal, they travel north. Our cities are the only way, save by boat, to cross the Therion River for over a hundred miles. No matter what name you choose to call them, it is undeniable they present a very real threat to all of us."

"You need not worry about your precious city. If anyone, Culler or otherwise, tries to break into Suriax, they will die long before reaching Aleria," Maerishka assured.

"And what of the refugees?" Mirerien asked. "If we were to send an escort to aid in their protection, would you object?"

"Fine, you may send your escort, via the wall, but should any of your soldiers set foot in the city, they will be subject to immediate arrest. Understood?" Mirerien nodded. Maerishka turned to leave, then stopped, a thought occurring to her. "He is with them, isn't he? That is why you are so concerned with a group of refugees from the Southern Plains." When they would have answered, she raised a hand. "Never mind, you may save your brother. I won't stop you, this time." With that, she left.

———

THE AIR WAS STILL. The trees and animals were quiet. Even the city was quiet. Maerishka looked up at the ramparts. Her guards stood rigid, at complete attention. They were disciplined, always vigilant in their duties, but today was different.

She shook off her unease and continued to her personal dock. On her order, the gate was opened, and a small ship sailed in. She waited as it was secured and Alvexton was escorted off. He smiled at seeing her and took her hand, flinching at the contact. Taking pity on him, she dropped his hand and pulled out a potion of fire and heat protection. He downed the liquid quickly and took her hand again, though it would be at least a minute before the potion took full effect. "What did you learn?" she asked as they walked hand and hand from the beach.

"I think the Alerians may be right."

Maerishka grimaced. Shortly after the first report from her cinder unit, Alvexton expressed a desire to go to the Southern Plains and personally lead recovery efforts for his people. The Southern Plains were his territory before their marriage. It was only right he should take a hands-on role in their protection and assessing future threat levels.

With all reports indicating the raiders were gone from there, she agreed. Given their continued presence in the Alerian territories south of Suriax, she insisted he travel by the Therion River. The river stretched for hundreds of miles in either direction, bisecting the sister cities of Suriax and Aleria. It ran east, through the Eastern Ridge, and travelled south, through Suriaxian territory. The way was not easy. Only an expert captain could pilot a ship through the treacherous mountain passes. Once past the mountain, the river ran all the way to Lerein, the capital of the Plains, but to see the areas deeper in his territory it was necessary to anchor the ship and ride by hound. It was a hard journey, but he seemed no worse for the wear.

"The destruction was unbelievable. I only went to a few of the places hit, but they were all the same. Nothing and no one was left. The fact that we had any survivors is a miracle. I thought to help with recovery, but there is nothing to recover. Any village attacked is gone. All the other towns and settlements are frightened but otherwise untouched. It was as if a massive storm swept through and then left. I have never seen anything like it before. If they are, in fact, traveling in this direction, we need to prepare."

"My people are not simple farmers. They can handle anything this horde has to offer," she offered indignantly.

Instead of getting insulted by the comparison, he patted her hand reassuringly. "I would never underestimate the strength of the people of Suriax. The truth remains that the city is still recovering from the Fire. Followers of Ferogid continue to hover around. Tensions are high. Random fights break out as those once weak now vie for dominance. An attack at this point could very well dissolve all of the progress the city has made."

Maerishka took in all he said, looking around her city as they walked back to the palace. Maybe he had a point. Suffering more loss of life and property so soon after rebuilding would add a tremendous amount of stress to their lives. They were already feeling it. Of course, they did not know exactly what was happening, but there were rumors, and those could be more dangerous than truth. Those who knew nothing could still feel the tension. They were nervous, on edge, and most did not know why. Stopping mid-step, she turned to her guards. "Assemble the city. I make an announcement at midday today."

———

She watched her citizens assemble in the great stadium tree. The entire city was shut down, save for the guards at the wall, but they already knew what she would say. She practiced her speech on them. Despite the thousands of people gathered in the tree, conversation was kept down to nervous whispers. She stood on her balcony, and even that stopped. Every man, woman, and child anxiously awaited what she would say. Taking a deep breath, she began.

"Citizens of Suriax, I come to you today with news of a possible threat to our city. As many of you know, the people of the Southern Plains have suffered greatly from a series of raids on their cities. These attacks were brutal. In all but a couple of isolated incidents, there were no survivors. Any village touched was completely destroyed.

"The raiders continue to travel north. They are currently in the Alerian territories to our south. Every indication is they intend to come this way. While I do not anticipate they will be able to get past the wall, their numbers are great, and their skill in destruction is undeniable. If we do find ourselves under a prolonged siege, it is possible, however unlikely, we could find ourselves fighting a battle within the city walls. Should that occur, boats will be waiting at the docks to transport anyone unable to fight due to age or infirmity.

"There is one more thing you should know. There are those who believe these raiders are, in fact, an organized band or army of Cullers." There was an audible gasp from the crowd. "I know what you are thinking. I do not know if these rumors are true. I can tell you the raiders are strong, difficult to kill, and relentless. Whether they are monsters from our past or an entirely new kind of monster is irrelevant. They enjoy attacking villages of helpless farmers in the dark of night, while their victims sleep. We will not prove so easy a target. And if they survive their battle with us, they will know never to challenge our strength again." Cheers rang up from the crowd. She waited a moment to let their excitement build, then held up her hand for silence.

"Take this time to make whatever preparations you deem necessary for you and your families. Thank you." Inclining her head to the crowd, Maerishka returned to her chamber. The tree, quiet before, was a hive of activity and sounds.

"You did well," Alvexton said, taking her hands.

She agreed. The tension of this morning was replaced by excitement and planning. The biggest problem with any disaster was its unexpectedness. They were all caught off guard and unprepared on the Night of Blue Fire. That would not happen this time. Let the raiders come. Suriax would be ready.

————

IT WAS TOO EASY, sometimes. Ridikquelass accepted an apple from the street vendor and munched on her snack while she walked around the city. So, this was Suriax. It was big, as she expected. Across the street, boys sparred, their hands covered in blue flames. She watched the practice with excitement. They moved with fluid grace and strength, throwing off small balls of fire at each other with every punch and kick. One boy picked up a shield, as his opponent's attacks grew too much. The stronger boy laughed and pulled all the fire to one fist, concentrating its heat to his knuckles, and punched. The shield shattered. The boy fell. In battle, this would be the time when the stronger fighter pressed his advantage and destroyed his adversary. This was not a battle. The weaker boy raised a supplicating hand and was helped to his feet. The stronger boy then proceeded to show the other boy how to perform that focused fire punch.

Ridikquelass wandered around some more. Everyone was busy preparing. They thought to ready themselves against attack. She almost laughed out loud. Instead, she tossed her apple core into a trash barrel and sat down at a small diner. She decided she wanted a glass of warm tea. Elves did make the best tea, after all. She should enjoy some before the city was destroyed.

The waitress brought out a glass of water and added the herbs at her table. Holding the glass with both hands, her palms began to glow blue. The water in the glass bubbled with heat. Once satisfied the temperature was right, the woman set down the drink and walked away. She blew on her tea and sipped it carefully. Perfect.

"Having fun?" a voice said, close to her ear. A woman with long dark hair and a simple dress sat down across from her. If not for the conch shell pendant hanging around her neck, even Ridikquelass would have difficulty recognizing her.

"Careful, Nadda, don't want anyone noticing your little voice trick. They may become suspicious."

Nadda shrugged. Resuming her mute act, she motioned for Ridikquelass to give her report. She took another sip of tea and was rewarded by Nadda's look of annoyed impatience. "Okay," she said at last, keeping her tone low. "So, we were right about the people in the caves. That Suriaxian woman from the Tyne-rock raid is with them. If we intercept them before they reach the city, we can snag her, although I don't know if we should even bother. Everyone here can do that blue fire trick. Some are probably even stronger than she is."

Nadda nodded. Standing, she waited for Ridikquelass to

follow her. Getting into the city was a simple task. They came in through the main entrance by claiming to be evacuees from the south. Not wanting to risk leaving the same way they came in and arousing suspicions, why would evacuees leave so soon with the warning of danger approaching, they moved to the southern wall and slipped out through a small tunnel left under the wall by some animal. They found it and three other similar weak spots unnoticed around the perimeter on their initial search of the city. Soon they would be back, and Suriax would fall.

———

"ARE you sure we didn't walk past Suriax and Aleria?" Marcy asked.

Thomas laughed. "Cheer up. If we did, we can just keep going until we get to my old home up north." Marcy rolled her eyes.

"We didn't pass them," Rand assured everyone.

"Is your mother a good cook?" Kern asked Thomas, ignoring Rand. "Because I am really in the mood for good stew and ale."

"We did not pass Suriax," Rand repeated.

"As long as we don't pass your home too and end up walking all the way to the desert settlements," Zanden said, adding his two coppers to their hypothetical discussion.

"We did not pass Suriax," Rand said again."

Lynnalin patted him softly on the arm. "Sorry, but no one is listening to you."

"Hrmph," Rand huffed and crossed his arms. "Maybe next time we get stuck in a mountain I will leave all of you to find your own way out," he grumbled. They all laughed. The mood lightened, they walked in silence again for a while.

Kern stared forward, stared at his feet, counted the knots in the wall and the cracks in the floor, anything to pass the time. The caves could be beautiful, but after spending so much time in them, he longed for open air. Looking at the walls, he noticed patterns he had not seen earlier. Small patches of moss-covered spots of the wall and floor. A small lizard slithered off into a crevice between the rocks.

"Hey, Lynn, did you add more light balls?"

"No, why?" she answered.

"Is it just me, or is it lighter in the tunnel?"

"No, you're right," Marcy agreed.

Barely able to contain their excitement, they hurried around the curves of the tunnel and were rewarded with the sight of daylight streaming in to an expansive, open cave. There were cries of joy, laughter, and cheers, as the other people in their group saw the sunlight. Kern stepped forward, blinking against the brightness of the light. Across the wheat fields, maybe a mile away, was the high wall of Suriax.

"Told you we didn't pass it."

EIGHT

"THEY ARE THROUGH THE MOUNTAINS!" PIELERE CRIED out, taken off guard by the flood of excitement, relief, and joy he felt coming from the survivors of Tynerock and Everend. "Sorry," he apologized for his outburst. He couldn't get the smile off his face.

"Don't be," Mirerien assured him. "I feel it, too."

"They are very happy," Eirae agreed.

"You, too?" Pielere asked.

"Not as strongly as you, if that goofy grin of yours is any indication. But yes, I do feel it, too. We should get everyone ready to move."

They opted to stay at the wall while they waited. Not knowing when the refugees would arrive, they had not wanted to waste supplies on a prolonged camp out at the foot of the mountains. Also, should the Cullers arrive first, they did not want to be caught by surprise, stranded away from reinforcements and drawing attention to their position. "If we hurry, we can get everyone over here before ..." he never finished his thought. The wall shook with a loud bang. They ran to the side

95

to see what happened. Soldiers moved in all directions, yelling orders and assessing damage, a large chunk of stone was missing from the top of the parapet. A boulder the size of a man sat just inside the treeline, a path carved out where it landed.

Pielere looked over the wall, but he saw no army, only a small bird in the sky. As he watched, the black dot he thought to be a bird moved closer and grew larger. "Take cover," he called. The wall shook again, this time from a much lower hit. Pielere felt the stone beneath his feet shift and sink, the stone falling to fill the hole left by the second boulder. A soldier moved and began to fall through as the stones shifted again. Pielere reached out, grabbed the man's arm, and pulled him out of the hole. Together, they crawled to a more stable portion of the wall. No spot was safe, however. Boulders continued to rain down on the city, destroying large segments of the wall and many of the buildings in the vicinity. Pielere felt fear, not his own, and swung his gaze to the mountains. Boulders, like those hitting Suriax, pounded the mountainside. Stones fell all around the cave opening. In his mind, he heard the screams of frightened children. In that moment he could see the scene play out. He saw the uncertainty and confusion. Should they go back into the caves and face being buried alive or run out into the open and face the monsters now clearly visible over the horizon. Several of the children ran outside, too afraid of the falling rocks to listen to the adults who called them back, and the decision was made.

Dodging boulders and soldiers, Pielere ran to the tower stairwell. Without a word, Mirerien and Eirae followed on his heels. They did not wait for their own troops, trusting their men to follow when they were able.

Pielere ran full speed, keeping one eye on the children and one on the approaching mass. Dozens of people flowed out of the caves. They ran erratically, desperate to avoid the boulders, arrows and other weapons now being thrown their way. Out the corner of his eye, he saw a large shape of a man, easily towering two heads above the other Cullers, lift another massive boulder to throw their way. Taking two quick moments to pinpoint the projected landing in the midst of a cluster of children, Pielere ran to place himself directly in front of where the stone would hit and stabbed his sword into the ground, raising his arms high. The boulder slowed directly above his head, as though caught by an invisible net, and stopped mid-air a few feet above the heads of the children. Then it began to move again, this time back up like a sling-shot into the Cullers, punching a nice sized hole in their ranks.

The refugees stopped moving, out of shock. If only the Cullers would do the same. The show only excited them more. The barrage of rocks and arrows intensified. This time all the projectiles stopped still in the air and fell to the ground the moment they impacted Pielere's protective barrier. Just when he thought his charges would remain still forever, Mirerien and Eirae caught up and gathered everyone behind him.

"Nice trick," Kern said in greeting. "Can you do that while moving?"

"I do not believe so," Pielere answered through clenched teeth, already feeling the strain on his impromptu wall.

"How long do you think you will be able to keep it up?" Mirerien asked.

"I do not know."

"Then we should get moving while we still have a small space between us and them," Eirae reasoned. "The closer we get to the city, the closer we are to reinforcements." Their soldiers ran to join them, but it would be a close race to determine who would get there first.

"Save my children!" one woman cried. The other refugees

joined in the request. Whatever happened to them, they wanted the children to make it to safety.

Eirae looked around quickly, taking in the marenpaie hounds. There weren't enough to carry everyone, but there should be enough to make a difference. "Load the children on the hounds."

The dwarf in the group moved immediately to comply, whispering to the beasts. Slapping each on the rear, he sent them off. They ran like bolts of lightning for the city. Eirae sighed. Whatever else may happen, the children would make it to the wall, and hopefully, safety. The way things were going, that was not a guarantee. "Let's move," he called.

Pielere dropped his arms and grabbed his sword. With no further protection from long range attack, they ran.

———

Maerishka surveyed the damage and said a quick prayer of thanks it wasn't worse, yet. Thanks to her earlier warnings, most people who lived and worked near the southern wall had temporarily relocated to farther north in the city. Otherwise, the death toll from that initial bombardment would have been much worse.

With most of the raiders focused on the small band of refugees, the attacks on the city had paused. It wouldn't be for long. Once the refugees were either safe or dead, attention would shift back to Suriax. Gathering everyone she could to patch the holes in the wall, she sent Alvexton to oversee the boats. He was better with comforting people. She was better with battle. Should the boats need to evacuate, he would see that her people were led to safety. It was her job to ensure that never became necessary. "Status?" she called.

"Four large breaks, several smaller ones," an unusually tall half-elf answered. Maerishka recognized him as a lieutenant in the Royal Guard. His name was Camdon. He was some kind of descendant of the desert elves, if memory served. His olive skin tone and sand-colored hair certainly supported that claim. "Only three reported casualties so far. Thirteen confirmed injuries severe enough to require healers. The clerics are currently treating the injured in order of severity."

"Good. See what shield spells we can get to strengthen the weak portions of the wall. Set up a kill box at any spot too damaged to repair or reinforce. I want our best burners to create a blue fire trap for any who get through. Station archers on all the roofs up to a block away from the wall, and have the mages put protection spells on everyone they can, priority on the melee fighters."

"Yes, Your Majesty." The man bowed and ran off to implement her commands. She heard a cheer of excitement and ran over to a group of smiling soldiers lifting children off the backs of Marenpaie hounds. The last hound came through the open door. Once inside, the door was closed immediately and bolted tight. The children clung tightly to the soldiers who held them. One ran over to Maerishka and would have hugged her legs if not for the timely intervention of a royal guard who scooped up the little girl. Maerishka nodded her head in thanks. She had no desire to burn the child with her heat.

The wall shook from renewed hits. "Have the children taken to the docks," she commanded. The sounds of battle grew closer. Grabbing on to a rope ladder on the wall, Maerishka climbed. Being on the wall was not the safest place to be, but she needed to see what was happening out there. She made it to the top and ducked to avoid a rock flying just overhead. The remaining refugees ran, besieged by the outer bands of the Culler army. There was no more denying who they faced.

Monsters covered in glints of metal pulled carts filled to the brim with boulders from the foothills of the mountains. Huge men, easily over eight feet in height and some nearly the same size in width, hurtled the boulders forward, having little difficulty throwing them the great distance. The men screamed and called out in excitement and battle fervor, crazed movements that belied no sense of care for the arrows striking down their comrades. They were not even hampered by the lack of limbs which afflicted a great number of them. They fought with swords attached to stumps and wooden legs embedded with enough spikes to mirror a mace.

Alerian troops fought and fell. Shining blue weapons and flares of magic were visible from her team. But there was only so much they could do to fight while running full speed to the wall. Without help, they stood a poor chance of making it. "Archers and long-range casters, give them support," she called. "Let us give them some breathing room."

The relief was instantaneous. Only kill shots made a difference. Lesser hits did not slow the monsters, but her people were skilled. Maerishka felt the wind from another boulder flying past and turned her attention back to the center of the approaching army. While many were running to intercept the refugees, others traveled at a more controlled pace in a direct line to the city. The mass of fighters, at first compact, now fanned out into a great black shadow. Sunlight glinted off metal shards and blades protruding from their bodies. They stretched out further, and she saw they meant to attack the entire wall at once. There would be no focusing on single spots of entry they could exploit. They intended to tear down the entire wall. And in that moment, she thought they could do it.

Fire burned in her chest, and she felt her fear melt into it. Removing her gloves, she tossed them to the ground. Fire sprung from her fingers. Concentrating, she made the flames swirl into a giant mass of blue and white heat. Her hair rose from the kinetic energy it generated. Taking a breath, she sent the ball flying into the mass of men. Without pause, she made another, then another, throwing fire like they threw boulders. Every ball took out three to four of them. It was not much, but it was the best she could do at this distance.

She continued her attack, encouraged by every man she saw reduced to ash. Drawn by the spectacle of her power, all but a few handfuls of men dropped their pursuit on the refugees. They were focused on her, now. Boulders hit the walls around her. She laughed at their inability to hit her directly until she realized their strategy. Her men called out a warning. It came too late. All at once the stone disappeared from under her feet. She fell through the rubble. Jagged rocks fell in all around her. She felt their weight on top of her. Small rays of light barely penetrated into the darkness.

She thought she must have lost consciousness, for when she woke it was to see the stone rubble lifted off of her by several sets of hands. Vision still blurry, she accepted one of the outstretched hands without thought and let herself be pulled to a standing position. Only then did she see the owner of the hand, Pielere, and realize he was unaffected from touching her. Confused, she pulled back her hand. It took powerful magic to resist the heat from direct contact with her skin. Even more confusing was why he helped her in the first place. The downward swing of an axe from one of the Cullers, now at the wall, distracted her from her questions. The axe, which was on a direct track to hit Maerishka, was stopped by Pielere's sword.

"Queen Maerishka," Pielere said, continuing to fight back the man. "We respectfully request entrance to Suriax for ourselves and our citizens."

A blue plume of fire shot over his shoulder and killed the man he fought. "Granted."

If only it were that easy. Refugees crawled one at a time

through a small break in the wall. It was a slow process. The rocks were hard and sharp, and a wrong move could cause everything to collapse. Soldiers from Suriax and Aleria helped lift the people through the hole. A couple of minutes, and they would all be through, if they survived that long. Of course, then there was the question of how safe the city was with Cullers already breaching the wall, taking advantage of similar cracks and breaks. But there was nothing she could do about that, now, except kill as many as she could before they had a chance to make it inside.

Dropping down, Maerishka touched her hands to the ground and reached out, drying any hint of moisture she felt. She boiled it right out of the soil. Small pockets of air burst through the surface, creating puffs of dirt, unnoticed by the enemy. Once she was confident the ground was as dry and brittle as it could be, Maerishka used her connection to raise the heat, cracking the top of the ground. Following the cracks and empty tunnels of air in the ground, she fed in her fire. The ground cracked more, parts of it caving in. Flames sprung out of every crevice, burning legs and feet. As they fell, their bodies came in contact with the ground, her ground. Each one burned as it was boiled from the inside.

In a normal battle, such an atrocious attack would demoralize the remaining troops, but they barely spared a glance at their comrades who writhed in agony on the ground. Standing, Maerishka opted for a change in tactics. Taking stock of everyone on her side, she used a pile of rubble to spring above their heads and sent out a fire claw, a giant half circle of fire focused to an ultra-hot blade's edge. The claw travelled outward in a cone, gaining width as it moved. The heat generated by focusing the flames to such a thin line enabled it to easily cut through anything it touched. Several heads, torsos, and legs fell to the ground for the next fifty feet. It didn't kill all of them, but it did temporarily disable those it did not kill outright. And many of those who lived found themselves trampled by other Cullers moving to take their place.

Beside her, Pielere and Eirae fended off attacks with deadly accuracy. They fought together, each completely aware of the other at all times. Their swords passed within inches of each other as they took turns hitting their shared opponents. For each Culler, Pielere would take a stab and swing around to hit another while Eirae hit the first man again. It was an interesting strategy that left their opponents unable to predict where the next hit would come from and decide who they should hit back.

Behind them, Mirerien launched arrows at those further back, thinning out the masses of support to relieve some of the pressure on the front lines. Further still stood Lynnalin, Rand, Zanden and Casther, her Cinder team. Each of the fighters had Suriaxian fire surrounding their weapons: Casther his sword, Rand his hammer, and Zanden his fists. Although Zanden was excellent with many weapons, his training and competitive fighting career led him to favor hand to hand combat. She was inclined to agree with his choice. He was the best.

All three men followed a strategy of taking out one or two men then stepping aside to allow Lynnalin to use her more powerful spells to kill additional men. Once her magic subsided, they jumped right back in, fighting until she was ready to cast her next spell.

That left three other fighters of note in this battle by the wall. One was a Suriaxian woman. The other two were former Flame Guardsmen. The woman called impressive walls of fire around the perimeter of the fighting. The two men fought with skill and precision, killing many men with a single strike to the head or heart. One of the men, her newly discovered half-brother, did not appear to be at all hampered by his lack of the Suriaxian fire he so willingly gave up. As she watched, he slid his sword across an exposed throat, ripping out the man's jugular and leaving him to bleed out on the ground at his feet. Kern looked around and called out a warning to Mirerien, his full sister. Dodging around the other fighters, he reached her just in time to take an axe hit meant for her. The weapon buried itself in his back, all the way to the wooden handle. Mirerien dropped her bow and held his limp body. The man who threw the axe was roasted by one of Lynnalin's massive, magic-enhanced fireballs.

"The civilians are through," someone yelled.

"Everyone inside," she heard another call. Raising a massive wall of flames to cover their exit, Maerishka retreated.

NINE

SURIAX WAS IN CHAOS. SOLDIERS AND GUARDSMEN SHOT
an endless array of arrows, magic, and fire at the invading army.
In some spots they were successful. A hundred feet to the west,
the wall exploded into a pile of useless debris. Marcy looked for
another boulder, as the source of the damage. Instead, she saw a
giant fist pull back from the dust. Cullers flowed in through the
opening. Many were picked off by the soldiers. Many others
ran past, deeper into the city.

Marcy continued running, led on by the steady pressure of
Thomas' hand on her arm. Without it, she did not know what
she would do. Kern's body hung lifeless over Eirae's shoulder.
She did not know if he lived, but given the reaction from his
sister Mirerien, it seemed unlikely. She was similarly led on by
her brother Pielere. Rand guided their unlikely group to the
marenpaie stables, flagging them all inside before securing the
doors. The refugees continued on with the soldiers. It was now
their job to lead the people to someplace safer, farther from the
battle.

It was strangely quiet in the stables. The walls were thick

and strong, made to stand up to the abuse of young Marenpaie still in training. Rand was the lead hound handler and trainer in the city. He knew this building and the hounds like no one else, making it a very good place to catch their bearings and develop a plan. And if the building was attacked, there were at least a couple dozen adolescent and adult hounds that would be good additions in a fight.

Rand cleared a cot near the back of a small office, and Eirae laid Kern down. Mirerien began crying without preamble. If Marcy expected them to check him over, treat his injuries, or try healing potions or spells, she was disappointed. They all simply stood around his body stoically, as though they knew he was gone.

Marcy felt her own tears bubble up. She grabbed Thomas' arm tighter and turned away, unable to look at the cot or the devastated monarchs any longer. Across the room, the others availed themselves of bandages and salves from the emergency treatment supplies. Using the reflection from a well-shined shield, Queen Maerishka tended a deep gash on her forehead. The lighting was poor, and her reflection was distorted, but there was no one else who could help her without burning themselves in the process. Her anger and lack of concentration made such a task particularly dangerous at this moment. Her heat was noticeable across the room.

Rand climbed down from the roof access ladder and jumped to the floor. "The fires are spreading in the west," he reported. "It looks like they are just south of Merchant's Square."

Maerishka put down the salve and looked to her people. "Zanden, take your team to the Square. Coordinate our attack there. We must keep them from the docks until evacuations are complete. I need to get back to the palace and coordinate our defenses."

They were mostly silent as Rand saddled the hounds and went back to the roof to check for the safest routes. Lynnalin used her last fire protection spell to protect Maerishka's mount from being injured by the close contact. Splitting up into two groups, the royals heading east to the palace and everyone else going west, they left.

They westward group rode in two-person teams. Marcy, Lynnalin, and Casther shot fire at the Cullers they passed. Thomas, Rand, and Zanden focused on getting them to the front lines as quickly as possible. The Cullers found themselves repelled, not just by the soldiers and guards, but by the citizens as well. Suriax was unlike anything they had yet faced. That fact excited them to a frenzy. Some resorted to animalistic behavior, jumping on their prey and ripping limbs from their body. Smoke and dust filled the air. Buildings fell as giants over eight feet tall used their bodies as battering rams. And then there was the fire. Blue Suriaxian fire burned everywhere. The more powerful among them fought encircled in balls of flame. Hands, feet, and weapons glowed. The ground was littered with an almost equal number on both sides.

They made it to the Square and were immediately allowed to pass through the blockade. At the head of the resistance forces stood Sardon Barief, a former, undefeated champion from the Tournament of Fire, the most prestigious fighting tournament on the entire continent. Sardon was one of the most dangerous men in Suriax. The only possible exception was Zanden, the current champion from the Tournament. The two men conferred and started issuing commands, no hint of their former rivalry evident.

Merchant's Square, normally a peaceful area of commerce and the only regular interaction between citizens of the two cities, was now a war zone. Large walls surrounded the square, really not a square at all, but a small portion of land on either side of the river. Here alone, people could travel across the bridge freely without going through a guard tower. They only went through guard stations if they chose to exit or enter the Square.

It was also the location of the main dock for both Aleria and Suriax. The Therion River was the way by which a great deal of trade entered their region. Many items were bought and sold right in the Square. Today, the docks served a very different purpose. By the river's edge, frightened children were loaded onto boats and sent to what they hoped was safety. Looking at what they faced, it was difficult to believe any place could be safe again. Marcy tried to put that thought from her mind and focus on the attack orders being called out.

In what felt to be counter intuitive, the soldiers positioned themselves outside the wall. Normally it would be foolish to give up the safety of a wall, but the invaders already proved walls were of little resistance to them. If the troops waited inside, they would risk being crushed by falling stone as the walls were broken down around them. Taking their positions, they prepared for the next wave.

———

CANDICE RAN with the other children toward the dock. Her horse, Sunshine, ran off afraid when the rocks began falling at the entrance of the cave. She missed the horse. It was the one thing she had left from her father. She only hoped Sunshine made it to safety, or that her death would be quick.

The children cried as they waited. There were many people ahead of them, waiting to leave the city. From what she overheard, no one had expected the walls to be breached, so few people actually began evacuating prior to it happening. Only those who lived in close proximity to the southern wall took the precaution of waiting in northern portions of the city. Still, there weren't as many scared citizens evacuating as she expected to see. Most people stayed to fight.

The clash of swords and raised voices signaled the renewal of fighting at the Square wall. The children cried louder. How much longer would they be chased by monsters? People rushed the boats, some falling into the water in their haste. Others clogged the bridge to Aleria, hoping to find safety there. Candice scoffed at that idea. What led them to think Alerian walls were any stronger than Suriaxian walls? Both cities would fall, just like her home.

Candice watched the fighting through the large metal gates of the Square. No longer frightened by what she saw, Candice looked at the faces of the attackers, angry, crazed, mutilated monsters that they were. They did not fear death or shy away from damaging blows. They fought for the love of fighting and seemed just as happy in dying as they were alive. This was the ultimate battle for them. Here stood an opponent worth fighting, not some farm town they could wipe out with little effort. This was a challenge, and they loved it.

A face in the crowd caught her eye, and Candice gasped in shock. She thought the face belonged to her father, but that couldn't be. He fought with the monsters. He was one of them. The crowd shifted, and Candice lost sight of the man who could be her father. Without a thought, she ran toward the gate. No one stopped her. They were too busy trying to get away. She looked through the iron designs of the gate and tried to find him again. Beside her, the other gate was bashed in by the body of a soldier, tossed hard by one of the larger monsters. From the unusual bend in the soldier's neck, she could tell it was too late for him. Crawling over his still warm body, she slipped out of the Square and moved behind the soldiers, looking for her father. Then she saw him, locked in battle with Thomas, the nice man who protected her on the journey here. Her father's face contorted with emotions she never saw on it before. His clothes were bloody tatters. He fought, despite a broken bone protruding from his left arm. She hardly recognized the loving father she once knew.

Thomas knocked the hammer from her father's hands and moved to swing his sword with an arc that would likely kill her father instantly, and Candice screamed for him to stop. Much to her relief and horror, he did. In the moment he looked toward her, her father grabbed a sword from the ground and thrust it up and into Thomas' chest. She heard Marcy scream as Thomas fell to the ground. The monster who was her father turned his head, drawn by the sound of Candice's scream. His lips curled in a feral abomination of a grin. She felt the bile rise in her throat and nearly threw up. Then his eyes looked at her with curiosity and confusion, and she saw some hint of recognition. The tide of the fighting shifted, and the moment was lost, as he found himself pushed on to the next opponent. Candice called after him again and would have followed, heedless of her own safety, if not for the grip of strong arms pulling her back. "Let go!" she commanded. "I have to help my father."

"I'm sorry, little one," the man said, "but he isn't your father anymore."

Candice struggled against his arms and words. His grip held tight, but in the struggling his cloak shifted, exposing his head. Candice screamed. Bone grew through his skin, covering his head and trailing down his shoulder. "You're one of them," she cried.

"Not yet, but you will be," another voice said. A man approached them.

The man with the cloak and the bone growths drew his sword and pushed Candice back protectively. "I'd rather die."

"Your choice." The new man closed his eyes briefly then

opened them wide, all hint of humanity gone. Shadows of dust sprung up around him, taking his form until they created five exact replicas of the man. This man and his clones looked very similar to the first man. They each wore armor of bone that grew out of their own bodies, though the bone on the second man did not continue up to his head. Like the monsters, they had weapons within their arms, but these were organic, a part of their bodies, not forced into mutilated skin. In fact, these growths were almost beautiful. But the second man, with his clones, also wore new, grotesque additions that marred his once pristine form. Broken sword tips were shoved wherever there was flesh enough to hold them, along the protrusions of bone.

The first man kept an eye on each clone, watching for where the attack would come from. Sparing a glance back, he pushed her away. "Do yourself a favor, girl. Get out of here while you can. Forget your father. Once anyone falls to this madness, they cannot be saved," he said with a sad tone of acceptance. "Go!" He pushed her again.

Candice stumbled back and watched the man launch an attack at one of the clones. It disappeared on contact. That left five potential targets. Rock and wood fell down around her from a wheelbarrow thrown into the wall above her. Candice ducked and ran back down the line toward Marcy, who struggled to drag Thomas to safety. Candice ran to his other side and ducked under his arm, taking what weight she could carry. The smell of blood was strong. She felt it wet her face, but she did not flinch. This was all her fault. She felt his weight fall suddenly on her and stumbled, struggling to remain on her feet. His eyes were closed, his breathing shallow. She did not think they would be able to carry him any further when a man came up and lifted Thomas over his shoulder. Calling for them to follow, he led them from the battle.

———

Traxton saw the girl led away and breathed a sigh of relief. Now, he could really focus on the fight. Normally he loved battle, but not this time. Martiene was his friend. They trained together for years, took oaths of pain together and fought together. Now, he must kill his friend. Unfortunately, the decision to kill him was much easier than actually accomplishing the task. Because of his Sublinate training, Martiene held on to enough of his memory and skills to anticipate Traxton's attacks. His ability to switch between magic and fighting also made him very dangerous. Whenever Traxton got close, Martiene threw out another clone or changed the ground from stone to mud, anything to throw off his attack.

Beside them, Cullers broke through the soldier blockade and rammed the gate. It rattled loose on its hinges, half of them already ripped loose from the stone wall. Traxton pulled a second sword from the dead hands of a soldier at his feet and swung both blades around in circles. Martiene's eyes twinkled with excitement. With a single weapon, they were evenly matched. When Traxton picked up a second blade, he was undefeated. Martiene salivated at the chance to take out Traxton at his best and prove himself to be the strongest fighter. Pulling his own sword, Martiene launched headlong into attack.

What he may have lacked in skill, he made up for with ferocity. The two men clashed, blade to blade, blocking blows they could not dodge by deflecting them with their bone armor. Martiene fought close, trying to ram his newly bladed arms into Traxton wherever they could do damage. Alternating between the blade and his unnatural weapons, with the occasional spell thrown in, Martiene's fighting style was unpredictable. Traxton held strong, letting the moments of the battle flow into him. He and his blades were one. His blades flew around, crossing in front of Martiene's throat. Martiene grinned and jumped back, barely avoiding decapitation. A ruby red line of blood at each side of his neck spoke how close he came.

But Martiene was undeterred. He threw a plume of smoke up in Traxton's face and struck out. Temporarily blinded by the smoke stinging his eyes, Traxton avoided the blade by feel and sound. Dropping his blade and causing Traxton to do the same, Martiene ran them both into the wall. Stone collapsed around them. The metal gate creaked and collapsed, sending the area into chaos. Cullers flooded over the opening into the square. Pushed aside by the rush of people, Traxton waited until he came to a stop and threw some canteen water on his eyes to relieve the irritation. He looked around, now a good thirty feet from the gate. Martiene was nowhere to be seen.

———

"Stay down." Camdon led the refugees behind the mage school, toward the residential areas of the city. With most of the fighting to the west, it made more sense to go east, even if it was in the opposite direction of the docks. If they could make it to the private palace docks, they could possibly still get to safety.

He looked to the group of fifty or so refugees. Normally, asking so many to follow one man quietly would be an impossible task. But these refugees all lost their homes and many loved ones already. They knew what they faced, perhaps better than he did. Crouching low, hiding behind the many low stone walls that lined the streets here, they pushed on despite their obvious fatigue.

The air smelled of smoke. The soft crackling of fire was the only sound nearby. The fighting in the other parts of the city was a distant roar. But he reflected as he stepped over another dead body, this one Suriaxian, they must proceed cautiously. The tide of fighting could shift over to them at any moment. Camdon walked past the dead body of an invader and stopped, struck by the burn marks on his face. Burns were by no means uncommon in Suriax, but these burns were different, precise. Three parallel lines were etched in the skin deliberately. Shaking off an uneasy feeling, Camdon kept walking.

The smell of smoke grew stronger as they drew closer to the gate by the palace docks. He pulled out his key, but it was unnecessary. The gate was open. A single push and it swung wide, banging loudly into the wall. Camdon looked around for any signs of life, but there was only death. Guards' bodies lie eviscerated, recognizable only by their uniforms. There was no sign of the one responsible. Camdon noticed the smell of burnt flesh and knelt by one of the bodies, examining the injuries. The man was covered in cauterized sword wounds. Camdon knew these injuries well. They were the kind left by a sword covered in Suriaxian fire.

"What is that," a refugee asked, pointing to one of the service buildings by the dock.

Camdon walked around to see what they referred to and did not know what to say. Still burning scorch marks stretched across the building in three parallel lines, just like the ones he saw on the body earlier.

A low laugh came from the other side of the building. A ding on the tin roof drew his gaze up to see a fellow guardsman crouched, still chuckling and grinning maniacally. The man launched off the roof, surrounding himself in blue fire while in mid-air, and landed on Camdon. The two men crashed to the ground and rolled down the beach.

Skin blistering, Camdon closed his eyes and rolled them into the river, knocking the guard loose and putting out the flames. He looked around for his sword and saw it on the ground where they fell. Before he could move to retrieve it, the man lunged out of the water and grabbed Camdon's leg, pulling him off his feet. Grabbing a hand full of sand, he threw it in the man's eye, using the distraction to break loose again.

"Here," one of the refugees called, tossing him his sword.

Camdon grabbed it and swung in one motion, easily disabling the rogue guard's arm. He only laughed. "What is wrong with you?" Camdon cried.

"Wrong? Wrong? Not wrong. Free. No rules or laws. Free to kill whoever I want, whenever I want. No reports or recorders or paperwork to file. No fees or politics or regulations. We are stronger than anyone in the world. We answer to no one. There is no right or wrong, just weak and strong." He began his maniacal laugh again, this time more of a cackle.

Camdon felt his eyes widen in horror. "You're mad!" But the man wasn't listening anymore. Lighting himself on fire again, he moved toward Camdon, stopping short when the fire went out suddenly. Looking down at his arms in surprise, he tried unsuccessfully to bring the fire back. Snarling in frustration, he pulled his sword and ran for Camdon. His swing fell lifeless, his body dropping to the ground. An arrow stuck out the back of his head. Water displaced by the approach of a large ship washed over the body and pulled it into the river. Camdon inclined his head in thanks to the archer at the ship's bow.

Grabbing some rope at the end of the dock, he tossed it up to the men on the vessel and helped to secure a ladder. "How many have you?" called King Alvexton. "Looks like five dozen."

"Nearly so, yes, Sir," Camdon answered.

The king sighed. "I fear we will not have room for everyone. This was the final ship to leave the Square just before it fell. We are stuffed to the brims here."

"If you can fit the women," one of the male refugees spoke

out, "we men will stay and fight." All the men added their agreement.

The king nodded and turned to one of the ship hands. "Load the women and make haste."

Many of the women were from Breakeren. They had no loved ones save perhaps the children already boarded earlier at Merchant's Square. But those women from the Alerian settlements cried at being separated from their husband's and brothers. Their men stood strong, never faltering in their resolve. They were happy knowing their women sailed to safety. Camdon watched them with a new sense of respect. He decided to give them a moment to watch the ship as it sailed away. Unfortunately, the raiders had other ideas a group of them breaking through the open gate and rushing the shore. Taking one last look at his ragged band of ill-armed farmers and craftsmen, Camdon held aloft his sword and ran into battle.

———

EVAN DROVE the sword into the man's chest and pulled free his bloody weapon. He lost his hammer, having lost it during his fight at the wall. Now, he had to make do with this scavenged sword until he could pick up another hammer. Without pause, he sunk the blade into the next person, willing his mind to clear. Her face was still present in his thoughts. He tried to lose himself in the battle, but he could not find the same release as before.

"What's wrong?" that small woman asked, jumping down from a fence post to stand before him. She was completely unconcerned by the battle, walking through it without fear. Then again, what had she to fear? None of the soldiers or civilians would attack someone who had the appearance of a little girl. Only the monsters he fought with knew how dangerous she was, and none of them were foolish enough to challenge her. Any who did wouldn't last very long. "You aren't having fun."

Evan continued to stab and dismember anyone who ventured too close, but she was right. He wasn't having fun anymore. "Help me?" he asked, longing for the blissful certainty and contentment he found before in his kills.

"Of course I'll help you, poor thing." She pulled him to his knee and patted his face reassuringly. "How about a mission, would that make you feel better?" He nodded, eager for something to focus on. The girl turned his face and pointed to the distant Alerian palace. "I want you to lead the attack on the palace. See if you can't capture one of the royal children, so we can share our freedom with them. Through the child, we will reach the parents, and through them, the nation. Everyone can learn our ways and become one of us. Wouldn't that be fun?"

He stood and grinned. Yes, that did sound fun. Calling to the men as he ran past, he headed for the palace, stopping only long enough to pick up a discarded hammer. This would be a lot of fun.

JAISTON LUNGED at his brother with a curved stick made out to be a sword. Emery ducked and jumped to avoid falling over their sister, Krylena. Their cousins, Pielere's five children, joined in and soon the room was full of wresting prepubescent three-quarter elves. Samantha watched their play and tried to release some of her tension. The sick feeling persisted, but she grew used to it. The royal families filtered into the adjoined chamber early that morning and stayed there the entire day. Long before word of the battle reached them, the younger children claimed nightmares and called for their fathers. Once details of the attack began to emerge, especially the impossible news that the wall of Suriax was breached, every moment became a struggle to keep the children from knowing how afraid the adults were.

The younger children were relatively easy to distract, except for those eerie moments of worry they felt, as though they knew something the rest of them could not feel or see. The older boys spent most of their time play fighting. They wished to join the troops and fight the invaders. One day this kingdom would belong to them. They wanted to defend it.

There were twenty of them in all: the eight children; Pielere and Eirae's wives, Traelene and Valesca; Mirerien's fiancé, Collin; four attendants; four guards; and Samantha. Traelene and Valesca sat by the window, keeping a watchful eye on the border wall. Samantha had to admit the two women were the exact opposite of what she expected after meeting their husbands. Valesca had hair as black as ink, pulled up in elegant braids. Her entire demeanor and attire bespoke a woman of royal tutelage. She maintained perfect posture with ease even after hours of sitting and waiting.

Pielere's wife, Traelene, was more of a wild woman. Bright red hair hung loose, unrestrained. Her clothes were vibrant greens and gold. She looked like a beautiful flower blooming from the forest floor. Indeed, Traelene came from the Great Forests, nestled in the heart of the northern parts of the Eastern Ridge. Protected on all sides by the mountains, they had very little interaction with outside settlements. Even the humans and dwarves who lived in and on the mountains rarely ventured into the depths of the trees.

Despite their differences, the two women were completely at ease with one another, speaking with a level of comfort and familiarity born out of years of interaction and mutual respect. They joked softly, trading stories about their husbands, but it was easy to see the worry behind their eyes. Traelene glanced her way, and Samantha quickly averted her gaze, too late. Uncomfortably, she walked to the far side of the room and leaned against the wall, staring at a corner. What was she doing here, anyway? What made King Pielere think she could be of any use to them? So what if she had feelings when evil men were near? It wasn't as though she could really do anything about it. A well-trained guard could watch for trouble and actually defend themselves and others should trouble arrive. If only she could fight.

"I'm Collin," Mirerien's fiancé said, holding a hand out in greeting. Samantha started. She had not heard him approach. He was a friendly looking man, with skin tanned and roughened from years in the sun. She could tell he was no courtly man, even if he seemed completely at ease in their company. For that, she was jealous.

"Samantha," she said, taking his hand. She followed his lead, taking a seat on a nearby bench. "I feel like such an intruder here," she confessed.

"I grew up in the palace," he told her. "My father was a weapons instructor here when we were all still children. Mirerien, Pielere, Eirae, and I grew up together." Leaning his elbows on his legs, Collin stared down at his hands, lost in the memories. "I studied with my father and watched him work with guards and members of the royal family. When he passed away, I was asked to take his place. Up until a few months ago, that was all I was. I guess I was always more than that, but still, being officially given access to the inner circle is an adjustment."

His story may have been intended to put her at ease, but all it did was make her feel more out of place. "I don't belong here," she told him. "I'm not family. I'm no one important."

"They say you can sense things. Is that correct?"

"I guess." Samantha felt the queasiness grow stronger. She looked in the direction of the window and felt an intense dread."

"What is it?" Collin asked, picking up on her mood shift.

"They're in Aleria." A knock sounded at the door, drawing everyone's attention but hers. Collin waited a moment before going to let the guard in. Even the children were quiet while they waited for the report.

Collin listened without comment then closed the door behind the guard and motioned for the royal wives to join him on the bench with Samantha. She tried not to squirm, being so close to everyone, and waited for what he would say. Collin looked her in the eyes and confirmed her feeling. "They broke through the border at Merchant's Square."

"What about Pielere and the others?" Traelene asked.

"No one knows. They were separated from their troops at the southern Suriaxian wall. No one is sure where they went after that, but they have not been seen near any of the fighting at our border. There is one more thing." He took a deep breath before continuing. "They believe Kern didn't make it. He was struck with a mortal injury just outside the wall. From all reports, he died instantly."

Samantha felt her own shock and grief mirror theirs. Kern saved her life. He was a good man, and the world would be a far darker place without him. The sickness in her belly intensified, and Samantha stood. All eyes turned to her, but she did not shirk from the attention this time. "They draw near," she said with confidence. "We must leave."

They followed her without question. Any other time she may have wondered at her ability to command such authority, but now was not that time. Kern protected her people whom he did not know. He led them through the mountains and saw them to the wall at the cost of his own life. She would see that his family made it to safety. Opening the entrance to the escape tunnel, she waited for everyone to file past, until all that remained were she and Collin.

He looked from her to the window and back. His expression was pained, his indecision clear. The woman he loved was lost in a battle zone. One brother was already dead. How much longer could she last out there? He wanted to find her, protect her, be with her in this time of pain, but he also felt a responsibility to her brothers' families. With danger approaching, he could not easily abandon them.

Overcome by an overwhelming abundance of hope and determination, Samantha put a hand on his arm and smiled. "Go to her. We will be safe in the tunnels. And should they follow, we will have the guards with us. Either way, we have a head start and perhaps an hour before they reach the palace. Warn the other guards and staff, and when you find the Lawgivers, tell them of our danger."

Collin looked at her with wonder, unhooking and handing her a sheathed sword from his belt. Samantha held the blade awkwardly, her confidence shaking slightly. "I'm afraid I don't have any skill with the blade." She handed it back, but he held up his hands, refusing to take it.

"I think when the time comes you will know how to use it."

"What do you mean?"

"It's just a feeling. I met someone with a gift like yours once before. He was a friend of my father's. The way you spoke just now reminded me of him. That sword belonged to him. I think you should have it."

"Thank you."

No longer conflicted, Collin saluted her in farewell and left the room. Holding her new sword, Samantha took to the dark escape route. The others waited for her at the landing of the initial staircase. There were several more stairways leading

AMANDA YOUNG & RAYMOND YOUNG JR.

down into the darkness. Pausing a moment to secure the sword to her person, she grabbed a torch from the wall and lit it on one carried by the guards. Valesca looked expectantly back up the stairs to the chamber. "He went to help the others," Samantha answered her unasked question.

With everyone present, one of the guards took the lead. The stairs curved around the center of the palace tree. As with all buildings of importance in Aleria, the palace was shaped by magic out of a massive tree. Hollow portions within the trunk formed the many rooms and hallways. Balconies sat nestled on the limbs. The walls, flooring and some seats were made from the wood of the tree. It was all very impressive to a human from the foothills.

Like the rest of the palace, the escape stairs formed from the wood of the trunk. They were narrow, only allowing one or two people to stand on each step. Every fifty to a hundred steps, the floor widened to a large resting area with knots for stools and an access door leading from other secure rooms throughout the palace. There was one such door hidden on every floor. Only the royal family and a few trusted guards knew the location of each door.

Eventually, the wood became mud. The air grew humid with water dripping on the floor at random intervals, and Samantha knew they were in the root system of the tree. The stairs here were made of stone, hand carved with a widening width the lower they went. The dripping of water was audible now. It echoed down the stairway. At last, they made it to the final step, eliciting a relieved sigh from everyone who crossed it. The group gathered in a wide cave at the center of several tunnels. The sound of rushing water could be heard in the darkness. Somewhere behind one of these walls was an underground river, fed from the Therion.

"Which way do we go?" Traelene asked.

Everyone turned to Samantha. "Does anyone know where the tunnels lead?" she asked.

"Some lead out of the city," one of the guards answered. "Others lead to similar access points within the city."

Samantha considered their options. As appealing as the idea of distance was, leaving the city also meant they were further from reinforcements. She thought back to the last time she spoke with the three lords. Pielere could feel the suffering of his people. Mirerien could sense where Kern was. They all seemed to possess strange powers. If they still lived, she knew they would find their wives and children. "What tunnels go south?"

"The one behind you leads to the healing clerics' tree," the guard answered. "The next one to the right lets out at the guard tower on the southern wall, just north of the river, and the one on the side goes south, but I don't know where it ends."

Samantha closed her eyes and said a prayer for guidance. She felt a tug on her chest, pulling her toward the clerics' tunnel. Needing no other sign, she turned that way.

TEN

"I'm sorry, Marcy." Bryce shook his head. Thomas rested on the grass, a rolled-up jacket for a pillow. Despite Bryce's bandaging, his wound continued to bleed. He coughed, and Marcy ran back to his side. Bryce stepped away uncomfortably. "What are you even doing back here?" he asked, not knowing what else to say or do.

"We went with Kern," she said, her voice breaking into a sob. "First Kern, now you," she cried into Thomas' shirt, unable to hold back her emotions any longer.

"Kern ... was hurt?" he asked hesitantly.

"Kern was killed at the wall," she swiped the tears from her red, swollen eyes.

"Oh, Marcy, I'm sorry." He put a hand on her shoulder, but she shrugged it off. Deciding to give her space, he turned his attention to the girl who was with Marcy when he found them. She sat with her back to the wall of the building they were hiding behind. Her eyes looked forward blankly, in some kind of shock. From what he overheard of her mumblings he could tell she somehow blamed herself for what happened, though he

124

couldn't fathom how. Knowing there was nothing else he could say for Marcy right now, he pulled the girl to her feet and led her around the side of the building.

"What's your name?" he asked, pulling a napkin from his pocket, folding it several times and handing it to her.

She looked down at the napkin, now a delicate white flower, and smiled, a look of complete innocence and wonder melting her face. "Candice," she answered.

Physically, he guessed she was about fifteen years old. Of course, he wasn't very good at judging human ages. Most people he knew had at least a little elf in them. Emotionally, she acted very much younger, at least at the moment. Then again, Suriaxian children tended to grow to maturity quickly, so maybe he was misjudging her. "Candice, it's nice to meet you. I'm Bryce. Where are you from?"

Her eyes shuttered slightly, but she answered, "Breakeren."

"Ah," he nodded, beginning to piece things together. "Is that where you met my sister?"

She shook her head. "We met in the forest when I was running. We've been running ever since."

Bryce closed his eyes and sighed. "Well, we will just have to see what we can do to change that," he said with more confidence than he felt. She smiled and seemed comforted. Now if only he could think of the right words to say to make things easier for his sister. "Come on," he said, standing. "Let's get back to Marcy."

———

MARCY HELD her hand over the bloody wound and felt tears run down her face. "Thomas, Thomas." She shook him, but he did not open his eyes. She felt his heart beat slowly under her fingers at his neck. His breathing was shallow. His chest rose only a fraction of an inch. She felt his life slipping away and looked around for help. There was none. They were alone with no potions or spells to heal his injury.

She sat up straight, her eyes wide. Spells. There was one chance, but it was risky with no guarantee of success. Looking down at his face, she made her decision and began to sing the song of binding. She only hoped she could remember all the words. There weren't many bindings in Suriax.

The ritual was created for King Emerien, the founder of Aleria. He was an elf in love with a human. Unable to imagine life without her, he had the clerics find a way to bind their lives. He shortened his life to extend hers. To be bound was a permanent choice, and it could not be done by force. Only true love could allow the magic to work. Only the willing could be bound.

Marcy sang and prayed. She prayed the gift of her life energy could save him. She did not know of any binding being attempted under such circumstances, but where magic was involved, anything could happen. And if she did cut her own life in half and lose him anyway, so be it.

She felt her palm warm over his wound. Her body grew heavy. Her head spun. She closed her eyes, feeling tired and weak. The sense of heaviness eased off, beginning at her head and peeling off her like a snake removing an old skin. She felt it last at her fingertips and toes. Then Thomas grew heavy in her arms. She opened her eyes, the dizziness gone, and watched as his features elongated into a more elven look. He took a deep breath, his eyes blinking several times. His hand went to his stomach. His fingers searched through the blood for an injury, but the skin was healed. He looked at Marcy, his clean hand wiping the tears from her face. His eyes searched hers. "What did you do?" he asked softly.

She leaned her face into his hand and cried quiet tears of relief. "We are joined. The magic of the binding saved you."

His eyes shone with gratitude and uncertainty. She could see he wanted to ask if she was certain she wanted this, but they both knew a binding would not work otherwise. He tilted his head, catching the distant sounds of battle with his newly heightened hearing. He stood and pulled her to her feet. "The battle is getting closer."

Marcy shook her head. "No, the sounds are as loud as before. You just couldn't hear it, then."

He looked at her in confusion and reached up to touch the soft points of his ears. His eyes grew with comprehension. "That will take some getting used to. Alright, well, we still need to move."

"Marce?" Bryce called out, looking between her and Thomas. Candice held onto his arm, holding a paper flower with her other hand. Her face glowed at seeing Thomas alive and standing. Bryce just looked confused. Then he saw the changes in their appearances, and the confusion turned to sadness. "Tell me you didn't."

"It was the only way," she defended.

Oblivious to the tension between them, Candice ran happily to Thomas. Laughing at her excitement, he knelt beside her. "Your ears look funny," she said, poking them. "Are you okay?" a hint of fear entered her voice at the question.

"Yes," he answered.

She hugged him tightly and cried. "I'm so glad. I thought my father killed you."

"Your father?" he pulled back to look at her face.

"I ... I didn't want you to get hurt. I just saw you two fighting and ... I know he's not my daddy anymore." She began sobbing into his still bloody shirt. "But what if he is? What if it is still him somehow?"

Thomas patted her back. Marcy and Bryce shared a look, their own argument seeming far less important given the pain of this young girl. "Come on," Bryce said to her instead. "I'll browbeat you later if we survive this mess."

"Wait," Thomas said, raising his ring to activate it.

"Kern's ring?" Marcy asked hesitantly. Thomas narrowed his eyes. "I think it's Frex, though he sounds strange."

"Frex? How?"

"Kern gave him another ring like ours before we left Aleria. It was set up to speak to Kern's ring first and only come to mine if the call went unanswered." He fell silent, listening closely. "He is in trouble, at the bakery. They are under attack."

"We must help him," Marcy said adamantly. With Kern gone, there was no one else to offer aide.

"Good luck with that," Bryce snorted. "I take it this bakery is in Aleria?"

"Yes," she answered. "It isn't too far from the main bridge."

"Wonderful. And how do you expect to get there through all the invaders and Alerian troops likely fighting to keep anyone and everyone from crossing into the city? And even if you can get over there, what makes you think you'll do it in time to actually be of any help?"

"I hate to say this," Thomas said, "but he has a point."

Marcy closed her eyes and grabbed her broach, as she often did while thinking. Only this time it burned her. "I think I have a way," she realized, holding on despite the heat. "My broach," she answered their questioning faces. "Feel this." She lifted it from her cloak for each of them to feel.

"Why is it so hot?" Bryce was the first to ask.

"And how is that going to help?" Thomas added.

"Lynnalin gave this to me as a gift," she explained to her brother. "She said it could have any number of spells on it. I felt it get warm like this once before when it activated a spell that allowed me to fall slowly. I think it wants to activate another spell. Come closer."

The moment they all were touching, the air shimmered and shifted. The bushes and ground turned to stone and over-turned tables and chairs. Three people attempted to put their weight against the door to keep it from being busted in. One, Marcy recognized as the baker's grandson, Alnerand. The baker, an older elven woman named Elisteen, and Frex, Kern's aged uncle, were no were to be seen. The man and woman helping Alnerand were much younger, though they dressed strikingly similar. Outside the Culler, invaders ran at the walls and windows. "Candice, get in the back," Marcy commanded, running forward. Bryce and Thomas went to help the others.

Pulling her heat in to her, Marcy sent it outward. The others flinched visibly as the wave passed through them and continued on outside. Once she felt the heat surround the building on all sides, Marcy sparked it, setting up a tall wall of fire around the entire building. Closing her eyes, she pictured the fire, watching it thicken and burn hotter. It was a death trap to any who entered it. Some still tried, but those who did make it through did not live long. Marcy kept feeding the fire heat until she felt her own skin begin to flush. "That's enough," she heard Thomas say. Inclined to agree with him, she tried to pull the heat back, but it was free now and did not want to be restrained.

Heat continued to rush out of her in waves, stealing her air and baking her skin. She felt her body falling, wrapped in something soft. Shocks of cold that she soon recognized as water helped break the hold the heat had on her. She opened her eyes, the pain down to a tingling in her fingertips and toes. Filling her lungs with welcomed oxygen, she took the glass of water Thomas offered her. Bryce beat a towel against the curtains to put out a small fire. There were singe marks everywhere. "Sorry," she coughed, struggling to sit.

"Don't be," the woman said. "That was quite a show."

"And it worked," the man added. "The streets are quiet again."

Marcy squinted, sure her ears or eyes were deceiving her. The man and woman sounded remarkably like Frex and Elisteen, but they were much too young. The man laughed and helped Marcy to stand. "I know. It's me. I promise. I've been getting younger ever since I returned to this city. I thought it was my imagination at first, state of mind and all that, but, well, there's no denying it anymore. Especially once it started happening to Eli, too." The couple shared a loving look and a chaste kiss on the cheek. Marcy smiled at their happiness. Whatever was at work here, it could not have happened to a nicer couple. Frex dedicated his entire life to keeping Kern safe in exile and hiding his royal lineage from those who may want to harm him. Now, Frex was given a second chance at that life. If only Kern could be here to see it. She felt her eyes moisten.

"By the way, where is Kern?" Frex asked, somehow tapping into her train of thoughts. "Not that I don't appreciate your help, I'm just eager to challenge my stubborn nephew to a wrestling match." His eyes twinkled with mirth.

"He is with his brothers and sister," Thomas jumped in, saving Marcy from having to break the sad news. She squeezed his hand in thanks for the rescue and sighed. They would have to tell him eventually, but it could wait a little bit.

"Who are you?" Alnerand asked, seeing Candice in the back of the shop.

"It's okay," Marcy assured her. "These are friends."

Alnerand walked over to her, coaxing her out of hiding. "I'm Alnerand."

"Candice," she replied, responding to his kindness and

youthfulness. Leaving the two of them to get acquainted, the rest of them developed their defenses. There was no chance of convincing Elisteen to leave her bakery, so the best they could do was have a plan in place for when the invaders returned. As the sounds of fighting grew louder again, they settled in for the next wave of battle.

————

"So, you are Kern, the man who plays with gods."

Kern opened his eyes and took in his surroundings. He found himself in a room, draped in red curtains, with shields and swords proudly on display. The room was comfortable yet efficient, with simple wooden furniture and a carpet made of grass. Across from him sat a man draped in a black tunic bound by a twisted golden cord. His armor rested on the floor beside his chair. A glistening black blade with ruby accents sat on the table to his other side. Kern knew without question this man was a warrior. Even without wearing his armor or weapon, he carried the air of a dangerous and lethal opponent.

"You reject the gifts of one and die saving another," the man continued. "You know it isn't every day a mortal sacrifices his life for one. Oh, of course, people die for their gods all the time in one war or another, but they never die from actually physically protecting one."

"One what?" Kern asked, still completely confused, having difficulty following the conversation. "Am I dead?"

"A god, and yes, you are dead, at least for the time being."

"But ..." Kern struggled to remember what happened before he woke up in this strange place. "I was protecting my sister."

"Exactly."

Kern tried to wrap his sluggish mind around what the man

said. "You are telling me my sister is a god?" he asked, finally making the connections.

The man put a hand on Kern's face, his fingers gripping Kern's chin. "Now you are getting it.

"Pielere and Eirae?"

"Also gods. They may be new gods, but gods nonetheless."

"That ... well, that explains a lot actually," Kern said, accepting the answer much quicker than he probably should. But it really did explain everything about how they acted and the powers they wielded. "And who are you?"

"First answer me one question. How is it you find it so easy to reject power? You rejected Venerith's gift of fire, which caused quite a stir by the way. And you reject any hint of mortal power or influence the Siblings try to give you. Why? What is it you desire?"

What did he desire? Kern asked himself that very question many times over the past few months. For years, his life made sense. He was an assassin, a mercenary. Then he found out he was of royal blood. His half-sister, Queen of Suriax, wanted to kill him. His full siblings were the rulers of Aleria. All four of them were beings of immense power: politically, magically, and otherwise. They were leaders, people whose actions shaped the world. Their choices mattered. They mattered. Who was he compared to all that?

The man looked at Kern expectantly. Not sure what he would say, Kern began speaking the thoughts in his mind, hoping his ramblings would lead to something meaningful. "I want to help people," he said honestly. "Leading the refugees was probably the first time in my life I really felt I was doing something I was meant to do. Before last summer, I never thought about what was right or just. But now ... when I found out there would be no reinforcements and the refugees were on their own, it felt wrong. I know Pielere and the others were doing everything they could, and I don't blame them. They had many other responsibilities to worry about, but when I looked in the eyes of the survivors, I knew I had to protect them.

"Suriax and Aleria are both so centered on the law. In Suriax, justice comes from the legal right to defend yourself and take revenge on those who wrong you. In Aleria, justice is about protecting the innocent and punishing the guilty. It's about maintaining order. But where was the justice for the refugees? Unable to defend themselves and too far from the protection of the cities, they fell through the cracks, lost and abandoned by both systems. They were victims of strategy and politics. There are some people laws cannot protect. There are some places the power of the law cannot reach. There are times the laws are less important than the lives of the people affected by them."

"Are you saying you, brother of the Three Lawgivers, do not believe in the law?" The man's excitement at the irony of that question was evident.

"No, it's important," Kern clarified. "But it is just one part of a bigger picture. Laws can be great. They can help people, but they are only as just as the people who write and enforce them. And even the best laws cannot help everyone."

"Couldn't you do more to help those people if you possessed greater power?"

"No," Kern answered adamantly." With power comes restriction, limitations. You have to do what is good for the whole and think about the big picture. You miss the individuals. I don't need power. I need freedom to act and go where I am needed, regardless of borders or politics or any of those other distractions. I want the freedom to do what is good and right because it is right. Just because something is legal doesn't make it good, and just because something is illegal doesn't make it wrong. I've been mired in laws my entire life, justifying my actions based on what was allowed and accepted in Suriax. Eirae opened my eyes to the error of that thinking. There is a higher moral imperative that supersedes the laws of any man. Without that guidepost, following the law is meaningless.

"Now, if I have efficiently answered all your questions, will you answer mine? Who are you?"

"I am known as Randik," he offered readily.

Kern felt his shock, surprised even more that he could still feel shock after all he recently discovered and witnessed. "You are the god of the Sublinates."

"I am."

"Well, then where are your followers? Shouldn't they be here, fighting their enemy?"

"The battle would be over before they could arrive. That battle will come, but trust me when I say you would not want it to take place over your home. As things now stand, the Cullers have a motivation to keep moving. Were I to send my army to this battle, that motivation would be greatly decreased."

"And what of all the homes they sack along the way to this final battle of yours?"

"I never said it would be the final battle, and there will be people who die no matter what any of us do. I cannot change that. With the intervention of people like you, some of those deaths may be prevented, but that is not something I have control over."

"And there is nothing you can do to help Aleria and Suriax?"

"So close to the seats of power for Venerith and your Lawgivers, no."

Kern sighed in frustration. "So, what happens, now?"

"Now, the Three Lawgivers awaken to their divinity, and things get interesting."

Kern heard the whisper of a voice and turned his head, but

the sound was impossible to pinpoint. No matter which way he turned, he could not locate the source. Other voices joined the first, and he felt a sense of familiarity, as though he should recognize them, but his mind was lethargic, cloudy. His chest warmed, his vision blurring to white at the edges. "What is happening?" he heard himself ask. His body felt weightless now. His field of vision continued to narrow.

"The birth of gods," he heard just before everything faded to white.

———

"Honestly," Maerishka complained, "I can't believe you brought the body with you." She looked in disdain at her former brother.

"Please," Eirae said. "It isn't as though you've never had a dead body in your palace before."

Pielere shot them both a look. Mirerien didn't notice any of it. She sat by Kern's side, stroking his hair as she had since they made it to the palace. "He is our balance," she said to herself. "He is an agent of good, the protector and the mediator, the light and the dark, the punisher and the punished. He who has walked both paths and chosen justice, not power."

Pielere and Eirae came to her side, drawn by the strength of her words. Eirae looked at his brother and sister with tears in his eyes. "Do you feel that, too?" he asked them, his voice raw, stripped of its normal sarcasm. They nodded. Without a word, they surrounded their brother's body and held out their hands.

"What are you going on about?" Maerishka asked, but they weren't listening. They closed their eyes then opened them again. Maerishka watched them with confusion. The air around them glowed. Their hands and eyes glowed.

Speaking as one, they said, "Kern Tygierrenon has been

judged and deemed worthy of another chance at life. His noble act of self-sacrifice has earned him this gift. So is our ruling. Let it be done."

The Three Lawgivers. That is the name people often used for the Alerian Lords. Maerishka felt a nervous energy in the pit of her stomach, like one might feel standing too close to a cliff's edge, as she watched the glow move from their bodies into Kern's. His chest rose in a deep breath, and the heaviness in the room eased at last. Maerishka couldn't believe her eyes. Kern sat up, struggling from the pain from his back injury, but alive.

"You couldn't have healed my back while you were at it," he joked, the gratitude plain on his face. Pielere laughed with relief and put a hand on Kern's shoulder. He sat up straighter almost at once, the pain gone from his expression. "Thanks," he said, rolling his shoulders experimentally. "Thanks."

"Thank you," Mirerien said, hugging her brother.

"This is all very touching, but how did you do that?" Maerishka asked impatiently.

"Well, that's an easy answer," Kern said for them. "They're gods."

ELEVEN

Before Maerishka could respond to Kern's absurd proclamation, the sound of giggling drew her attention. Standing on the small balcony overlooking the room was a small girl. She leaned her elbows against the railing, resting her head on one hand. Her ankles were crossed casually, and her curled dark ponytails bobbed with her laughter. "Gods, huh?" she said in a high-pitched voice. "This is going to be fun." She swept a calculating eye over each of them and stood, clapping her hands together. "I'll take the serious looking one. You can have the rest." Placing her hands flat on the railing, she easily went into a handstand and flipped off. Rebounding off the ground with a roll and jump, she spring boarded off Eirae's shoulder to land at the back of the room. Leaning forward, one hand under the opposite elbow, she extended her pointer finger and motioned for Eirae to follow her.

"I am not fighting a girl," he said indignantly.

"Oh," she pouted and drew a dagger, throwing it before anyone had time to react. It flew next to Kern's head, embedding itself in the back cushion of his seat. Instantly, five more blades appeared at her fingertips. "Should I keep going?" she asked sweetly. "I'm sure one of these will hit." Eirae growled and drew his sword. The girl smiled and closed her hand, putting away the blades. "Excellent. It's playtime." Turning, she ran from the room, Eirae close behind.

The rest of them did not have time to follow. A low growl and snort drew their attention behind them to the main chamber door. There stood a woman in a coat and top hat beside a very large Culler holding the chain of an equally large, wild drander. The man dropped the chain, and the drander ran in, scattering the group. The man followed his beast. Swinging a large hammer, he ran for Kern and Mirerien. Pielere was busy fending off the drander, trying his best to avoid being gored by the long tusks. He managed several hits, but most were blocked by the animal's boney armor.

The other two had their hands full with the Culler. With his size and large swing, a single hit could take them both out. Trying to get past his reach to strike with their weapons was nearly impossible, and the physical constraints of the room made Mirerien's skill with the bow relatively useless. Kern attempted to keep the man's attention to allow Mirerien a chance to take a more advantageous position, but he was aware of their strategy and refused to allow her that opening.

Maerishka turned to face the last of their intruders. The strangely dressed woman was not loud or talkative like the girl. She was not large or muscular like the man. She did not have a feral demeanor or cover herself in many weapons. Instead, she held a staff, which she tapped lightly against the floor in between a few light swings to the side. Short, dark hair peeked out from underneath her hat, and her coat flared out dramatically. This woman quietly demanded attention.

Without a word, she approached Maerishka, continuing to swing her staff. Maerishka called fire to her hands and shot small balls of flame at the woman. She easily avoided the attack and swung at Maerishka's legs. Maerishka did not jump out of the way but dropped and grabbed the staff, transferring her heat to the stick. She felt it travel up to the wood and to the woman's hands, but she held on tight, smiling.

"You think to stop me with pain?" the woman asked, without opening her lips.

Startled by the trick, Maerishka allowed the woman to pull back her staff and suffered a hit to the back of the head for her mistake. Angry, she launched into every attack she knew, both with fire and without. The woman avoided all of them. Quick and quiet, she was a phantom unaffected by pain or fear. Well, there was one pain no one was immune to. Reaching out, Maerishka grabbed the woman's arm and sent in her heat, boiling the blood from within. Normally, she would only touch a person for a moment to initiate this particular attack, but even after she saw the woman's features contort in pain and her fingers go slack around the staff, Maerishka continued to hold her arm, determined to make this death as painful as possible. She saw the woman's lips part, and Maerishka smiled. Then the woman took a breath and screamed.

Maerishka dropped the woman's arm and fell, hands clutching her ears at the inhuman screech that pierced through the room. She squeezed her eyes closed and willed the sound to stop, unable to move or think while it continued. When finally she could open her eyes, the woman was gone, though the ringing continued to impede her hearing. She saw Pielere and the others talking over the dead bodies of the man and drander, but she could not hear their words. Stumbling, her sense of balance gone, she fought against dizziness and nausea to stand. Svanteese ran into the room, drawn no doubt by the woman's scream, and helped her to a chair. "Cleric," she said, trying not to yell, but unable to tell if she was successful. Svanteese nodded and left to find a healer. Maerishka touched the blood dripping from her ear and closed her eyes to wait.

———

Eirae ducked as another dagger flew past. He still couldn't tell where they were coming from. Every time he thought he knew where she was, she moved. Even more impressive, she managed to retrieve her thrown daggers without being seen.

He followed her into the main ballroom. Surrounded on all sides by the circular balcony, stairs coming down in three spots, this was a playroom for someone like her. There were a hundred places she could hide, countless shadows and corners to exploit.

He felt a cut on his leg and looked down at the streak of blood there. "Can I at least know the name of my opponent?" he called, trying to draw her out.

The girl stepped forward from the shadows in front of him and gave a slight bow. "Ridikquelass," she announced. Her ponytails bobbed as she spoke. She held a curved blade in her hand, pressed regally to her chest. Then she stood straight and began walking around him in a wide circle. Her steps were deliberate, heels hitting hard and rolling to the toes. "You don't look like much of a god," she commented.

"Is that so?" He watched her steps, tracking the shadows without moving his head. Just a few more steps and she would be close enough. All he needed was to touch her for a second, and he could end this.

"Then again, maybe your children will be more fun. Demigods do develop in unusual ways, and they are rarely held by the same restrictions as their parents."

"You speak as though you have a great deal of knowledge on this subject." Two more steps, he counted.

"You'd be surprised what you can learn from people's minds."

She came around to his right, and Eirae reached out, brushing his finger against her arm before she could jump completely out of the way. It was enough. He felt his power go into that touch, encouraging her mind to develop a hallucination designed to bring out feelings of guilt and remorse for her past actions. It was an ability he discovered while interrogating prisoners and was very effective in getting confessions. He did not control the visions or even know what people saw, but he heard enough reactions of them to get a pretty good idea what they were like. It wasn't pleasant.

"Oohhh, do it again." The girl shook with excitement, catching him completely off guard. "Better yet, let me return the favor." She somersaulted over Eirae, reaching above her midair to touch him on top of his head. Her hair became a kaleidoscope of colors.

Eirae fell instantly into darkness. The walls melted into shadows. He tried to walk, but the floor was gone. He could not move. His body was trapped, surrounded by a thick, sticky cloud of fear and pain. He saw faces shift, translucent in the pitch-black void. His mother's face smiled then screamed. He saw her body and felt his anger at her death and at his father for causing her to die with his greed and corruption. The rage filled him, smothering him, and he was back in that moment, lost to his hate. He thought of all the things he would do to their father. He did not even care if he was arrested and executed for his actions. He would gladly accept any punishment if it meant his mother's death would be avenged.

He felt his brother and sister reach out to him, calming him, just as they had back then. This was all in the past, a memory that could not hurt him. Their father was long dead, a victim of his own machinations. Justice was found through the law, and the people of Aleria were freed from his corrupt reign. "So, this is why you weren't affected," Eirae mused aloud. "You have a similar ability to mine."

"One big difference," she responded, her voice coming from the darkness. "I'm in here with you." She giggled, and he felt the darkness press in tightly, searching his mind for another memory to exploit.

"Not going to work," he informed her. "You already found the worst moment of my life. Nothing else comes close. There isn't much else you can do to me." The inky darkness began to lighten to grey.

"Maybe not, but there is plenty to learn. You three really are gods, huh? He is going to love that."

"Who?" Eirae asked, searching for her mind. If she really was in here with him, maybe he could reverse the flow and see her secrets. In the grey mist around him, he saw a dark form take shape. It was the shadow of a large man with a broad chest and chains wrapped around his massive arms. Each arm was easily as wide as or larger than a normal man's head. Eirae could not see any details, but what he saw was enough to set his nerves on edge. He pushed for a clearer picture, but suddenly the shadow was gone, wiped clear away.

"Uh, uh, uh," the girl said. "No fair sneaking into my mind uninvited. You have no idea where it's been," she chastised with mock seriousness, or maybe it was actual seriousness. It was really difficult to tell with her. Before he could figure it out, a loud scream rang through the room, and he felt the hallucination fall away. The suddenness of it left him dizzy and momentarily confused. The girl stood in front of him with her hands together in front of her face. "Well, that is my cue to leave. Bye-bye." Leaning forward, she opened her hands palms up and blew sparkling gem dust in his face. By the time he cleared his eyes, she was gone.

Pielere pulled his sword from the heart of the now dead drander and looked up at Eirae approaching from the hallway. "Nice of you to join us," he quipped.

"Why are you sparkling?" Kern asked.

Eirae disgustedly dusted gem dust from his shirt. "That minx threw it on me right before she disappeared. What was that horrendous screech?'

"The one in the top hat," Kern explained. "Oh wait, you didn't see her. There was a woman wearing a top hat," he repeated.

"That woman resisted my deadliest attack," Maerishka seethed, smoke rising from her chair wherever she touched it. The cleric healing her ears flinched in discomfort but did not complain.

"How's the ears?" Kern asked a little too cheerfully for her mood.

"If I ever get my hands on that woman again ..." The arm of her chair crumbled to ash under her hands before she could finish her threat. "Aren't you done, yet?" she demanded, throwing an angry look at the cleric.

"Almost, Your Majesty. The damage was quite severe. It is a wonder you can hear at all."

Pielere could believe it. His ears were still ringing, and he was across the room when the woman screamed. Her attack was potent. Pulling out a cloth, he wiped the blood from his sword and found himself looking north. He could sense trouble in the tunnels.

"We need to get to the border," Mirerien said, interrupting his thoughts. "I feel much death. We must rally morale and lead the defenses."

Normally the first to head into a fight, Eirae looked off, a pained expression on his face. "My children are afraid. They are in danger."

"As are mine," Pielere admitted, feeling his brother's dilemma.

"Ah, the joys of family," Maerishka taunted. "What will it be? Will you save your kingdom or your children? Gods or not, it would take all three of you to have any hope of stopping that army, unless you can be in two places at once."

"She's right," Kern said, surprising everyone. "I'll go. I can be at the palace in seconds."

"Are you sure?" Eirae asked, his expression relaxing.

"Of course. They are my family, too."

Mirerien went to Kern, giving him a hug for thanks and luck. "Just try to stay alive this time. I don't think we can bring you back again."

"Don't die. Got it."

"One more thing," Pielere said, putting a hand on Kern's shoulder. "They aren't at the palace. They are in the tunnels under the clerics' temple." Putting as much force as he could behind the location of his family, Pielere willed Kern to go there. A moment later, he was gone.

"Please," Maerishka scoffed. "You act as though you are the only ones with power. Touching her necklace with one hand, raising the other for dramatic flair, she said, "Logeaneportas." They were instantly teleported to the southern tower for the main bridge connecting the cities. She lowered her hand smugly. Four pearls on her necklace grew cloudy and dark, their magic spent.

"Thank you, Your Majesty," Pielere said politely. She rolled her eyes and threw a fireball at the first Culler she saw. Walking off, she began issuing orders to her men. "I think we may have outlived our welcome."

"She'll get over it," Eirae said. "Besides, I am ready to get back on Alerian soil. Do you think you can get us past that bridge?"

"Me? What about you two?" he teased. "I'm exhausted."

Eirae laughed. "Calm down, old man."

"We're the same age." Pielere pointed out.

Ignoring the response, Eirae took a step back and gave a small salute. "See you on the other side." Still laughing, Eirae disappeared.

"What about you?" he asked Mirerien.

She looked at him uncertainly. "I don't know if I can. I've never been as strong as the two of you."

Pielere took her hand and smiled. "Together?" She nodded.

The scene at the tower melted away, replaced by the view from the north side of the river. Eirae acknowledged their arrival and dismissed the guard he was speaking with, joining Pielere and Mirerien by the wall. "We have fighting breaking out all around the Square," he reported. "But that is as we expected. There are also significant skirmishes taking place at isolated spots throughout the city. The two of most importance are here, at the bridge, and over there, in the central shops area. So far, they have funneled the worst of the fighting away from the majority of homes, but if any of those three areas fall, it won't take long for the Cullers to fill the rest of the city."

"So, we have a battle on three fronts," Pielere summed up the report.

"And there are three of us," Mirerien added.

"I'll take the Square," Eirae volunteered.

"Which would you like?" Pielere asked Mirerien, leaving the choice up to her.

"I'll take the shops."

"Then the bridge is mine. Good luck to us all."

With that Eirae and Mirerien teleported to their spots, and Pielere took in his own scene. Cullers jammed the bridge, picked off by archers and mages. They were not the problem. Near the shore, other invaders jumped into the shallow water, coming to shore along the River wall. Larger men pounded fists into the stone, breaking out sections enough to crawl through or climb over. His people were doing a decent job of holding their own, but for every one Culler killed, two or three more came to take his place. He needed to plug the holes so his people could focus on the men already inside the city if they had any hope of survival.

A flash of light appeared on the southern side of the river. Blue fire stretched out a good fifty feet in both directions from the tower by the bridge. Maerishka was fighting a similar battle to stop those who left Suriax only to turn around and come back once the path to Aleria became bogged down by fighting. Those on the center of the bridge actually became so frustrated by the lack of opponents they began fighting amongst themselves. Several were pushed into the river, their spots quickly taken by those attempting to make it to either exit of the bridge.

Pielere looked at the center walkway crossing their entrance and thought back to the refugees. With the start of a plan, he walked to the center most spot. Guards cleared a path for him. "The Protector," some said in awe and surprise. Feelings of relief and excitement washed over him, giving him strength. They called him "The Protector," one of the Three Lawgivers. Kern said they were gods. If that were true, it was time he lived up to his name and the faith his people had in him. It was time he stood as protector of Aleria, her people and her laws.

Taking out his sword, he put the blade to the stone at his feet, as he had before, and stretched his awareness into the wall. Envisioning the wall as an impenetrable barrier, he was rewarded by feelings of shock and elation as his people realized the Cullers could no longer enter the city. Fed by the faith of those who realized he was the cause of the barrier, Pielere stretched the field further, to the entire length of their southern wall, around Merchant's Square and beyond. The more hope he felt from his people, the stronger and easier it became to maintain the wall. Finally, he opened his eyes, easily holding the wall with only a small portion of his concentration.

"*Show off,*" he heard Eirae's thoughts directed to him.

Pielere couldn't help grinning. "*Your turn, Brother,*" he challenged back. Taking one last moment to make sure the wall was stable, Pielere joined the fighting.

———

EIRAE TELEPORTED himself to a roof near the Square and jumped down to the ground. If anyone noticed his sudden appearance, they were too busy to think much about it. Slicing his sword into Cullers as he moved, Eirae took in the battle at a glance. Most of the conflict was still a spillover from the Square. A few made a break from the mass of bodies and swords to go further into Aleria, but most didn't realize they were in a new city. They were having too much fun where they were. In the Square, Alerians and Suriaxians fought side by side, united by their common cause and desire to isolate the invaders away from other parts of their cities.

He dispatched another invader and tried to contain his frustration. This was taking too long. In the time it took to kill one man, another three slipped past and were set loose on the citizens of Aleria. A pressure wave rushed through the air. At first faint, Eirae saw a glow of power strengthen along the border walls. The fighters did not notice right away, but its effects were quickly seen as Cullers were repeatedly repelled back from Aleria by the invisible force. Heartened by the aid, the men near the wall cheered and pressed attacks on their confused opponents. "*Show off*," Eirae thought to himself.

"*Your turn, Brother*," he heard Pielere think back.

Eirae cracked his neck and centered his energy. So Pielere, the Protector, wanted to raise a wall? Well, he had a name among the people as well. Opening his eyes, he sent out his mind, searching for those with even a sliver of conscience left in them. The pickings were small, but for those who did still possess a fraction of their minds, he struck, pulling on their remorse and leaving them to endure a mental torture of their own design. It was his first time ever attempting this without first touching the person, but it was not as difficult as he imagined. Some began ripping metal attachments from their flesh, as they sobbed and screamed in agony. A few were killed by one side or the other, but most were left alone as everyone had plenty of other adversaries to worry about.

In the order of punishments, first came remorse and contrition. This was his favored method for a person who was truly sorry for his crimes. Such a person would undergo far worse torture than anything Eirae could devise. It was also the most effective way to change a person and encourage better behavior in the future. But not everyone regretted the evil they did.

Next in the order of punishments was pain, either physical or emotional. Neither method was really appropriate here. The Cullers were unlike normal people. Those unaffected by his earlier attack would not be susceptible to any emotional pain he could imagine, and it was obvious from his interactions with them that physical pain also meant nothing to them. They would not be demoralized by the death of comrades, and they would not be dissuaded or discouraged by the loss of a limb.

That left the final punishment. For those who could not be reasoned with or contained and who posed an immediate and future threat to the lives of others, death was the only sentence that remained. Calmly, Eirae held his blade before him and placed a palm flat against its surface. He would be a sword for justice this day. Letting the strength and purity of the law guide him, he moved, dispensing death with a single strike of his sword or touch of his hand. All who faced him fell dead. As his men began to see this feat, they cheered, their own hits striking truer. Bolstered by their excitement, he moved faster. Some men began to fall as his hand waved near, without any physical contact.

He cut a swath through the Square, dispensing his justice to nearly two dozen invaders in the span of a minute. Despite the achievement, there were quite a few more than that yet to go. Drawing on the faith and encouragement of his people, he continued. This was going to be a long, dark battle. With night-fall upon them, the fighting would soon become more perilous. Catching sight of a dwarf and elven woman riding on maren-paie back, he jumped over broken fences and dead bodies to get closer to them. The dwarven man swung a bright blue, fire-covered hammer at men as he rode. The woman cast spells, both in protection of the dwarf and in offense. Her spells were also enhanced by Suriaxian fire. Both of them fought beside Kern and himself at the wall. They were skilled and to be respected for their continued fighting this long into the conflict. The woman was the first to notice him. "Impressive spell," she said, indicating the death touch he gave to a man attacking her.

"Do you have any light magic?" he asked without preamble, killing another man with his sword as he awaited her answer. "We need something bright enough to fight by," he explained at her confused expression."

"Oh." The woman dug through her bag. "*Solyle*," she said, a scroll disappearing into a ball of light at her hand, where it remained for a few seconds before shooting up into the sky.

The effect was instantaneous. Both sides of the Square lit up as bright as midday.

"How long will it last?"

"It will remain bright a short time, then in about half the time of a normal day, it will dim to darkness."

"Understood. Thank you. Where are Thomas and Marcy?" he asked, continuing to fight by their sides.

"Don't know," the dwarf grunted. "We saw him get hit just before the fighting spilled into the Square. Haven't seen either of them since."

There was no time for further conversation. The tide of battle was pulling them apart. Focusing on areas of the densest fighting, Eirae set about relieving the burden from as many of his troops as possible. This would still be a long battle, but at least now it would not be quite so dark.

TWELVE

THE TUNNELS WERE A MAZE, A CITY UNDER THE CITY.
Some opened up into expansive chambers with alcoves and
endless paths and corners to explore. Others led to dead ends or
cliffs overlooking enormous caverns. The rock in spots was
perilously slick, and the mothers were constantly after their
children to be careful and stay with the group. Samantha
couldn't blame their excitement. Even she wanted to go
exploring a few times, entranced by a particular outcropping of
rocks or inclines that led to partially hidden caves along the
walls. Only her nagging feeling of danger kept her excitement
and curiosity at bay.

At the next intersection of tunnels, they stopped while the
lead guard checked the carvings by each opening for the correct
path. It was a slow process, but at least it gave them a chance to
rest. Not every tunnel was marked, but they discovered a few
chambers back that some did have markings to indicate where
they led. Since no one in their group spent any significant time
in the tunnels before, other than in the immediate vicinity of
the palace, the markings were a welcomed find.

"This way," the man called at the third tunnel.

"Jaiston," Valesca called to her son. He had a bad habit of running off into dark corners and looking for unusual rocks or other treasures whenever they stopped. She called for him again with no answer.

"I'll look for him," Samantha volunteered. She had a pretty good idea where to start. Just before this chamber was a series of steps and caves all the children found fascinating. Her good spirit faded instantly away as the sound of loud footsteps and banging rang down the halls. The feeling of evil intensified. "You go on ahead. I'll find him and catch up." Valesca looked at her uncertainly, clinging to her other two children. Terror shone in her eyes. "I promise."

All but one of the guards went with the group. The other stayed with her. Together they searched, afraid to call out his name too loudly and be overheard by their pursuers. "Over there," the guard said at a soft tapping on the stone. They followed the sound to a small opening. Samantha peaked in and found a narrow tunnel slanting up. The tapping was louder in the tunnel. Climbing in, she handed the guard her torch and began crawling. With his armor, there was no way he could fit in the cramped space. It was a tight fit for her. The sword Collin gave her made crawling in the dark tunnel even more awkward, but she moved toward the sound, the approaching danger speeding her movements.

At last, she saw a dim light and the tunnel began to widen into a small cave. Jaiston sat on one side, striking rocks together to make fire for his impromptu camp. His treasure trove of rocks sat beside him on the floor. He looked up at her and smiled, proud to show off his secret space. "We need to go," she said softly. "The others are waiting for us."

"Okay," he said, reluctantly gathering his things.

Samantha began the crawl back down, acutely aware of

Jaiston's movements behind her. At the bottom of the tunnel, she saw the flickering of light from the guard's torches. Her heart pumped wildly in her chest, the feeling of time running out pressing hard on her. She heard footsteps shuffle, and the torchlight shook, going out. Samantha froze. Reaching back to grab Jaiston's arm, she silently bid him to remain quiet.

A soft glow reappeared at the bottom of the tunnel. A hand reached in, shining torch light up at them. It was followed by a head. A man, not the guard, looked up at them and smiled. He reached for Samantha, and she twisted around to kick at his hand. He laughed and reached again, pushing as far as he could into the narrow space. She kicked frantically and hit his torch arm. The torch fell, burning her leg before she kicked the flame out. Jaiston clung to her arms. The man grabbed at her feet. Pulled in two directions and struggling in the dark, she eventually lost the battle. The man got a good grip on her ankle and pulled her down.

She and Jaiston tumbled down and out into the chamber. She pulled Jaiston with her, holding on to him and shielding his body from the brunt of the fall. Back stinging from the hard contact with the stone floor, she pushed past the pain and stood, picking up the boy and running in the direction of the tunnel the others went down earlier. She ran by memory. It was pitch black, but somehow, she managed to get to the wall of tunnels before stopping. Feeling around for the path they took, she could hear and feel the man following them. He banged his weapon into the wall and floor, making as much noise as he could to frighten a response out of them. He made his way around the room, swinging his weapon, getting closer to them with every step. Samantha took small, quiet steps. Her free hand ran along the wall, feeling for the next tunnel. Finally, her hand hit air, and she turned down the dark void. Whether or not it was the correct path, she did not know, but she couldn't stay in that room any longer without great risk of being found. She heard the man pass their tunnel on his circuit of the room. Jaiston tucked his head in at her shoulders, his earlier bravado gone. In the darkness, there was no one to see the tears of fear she felt through her blouse. Holding him tightly, she continued down her dark path. She only prayed it was the right one.

———

"WE HAVE TO GO BACK," Valesca said, pacing the small chamber they were in. "It has been too long. They could be lost or ..." She stopped herself at the look of fear on her daughter's face. Kneeling before Krylena, she gently stroked the girl's hair behind her ear and put on a brave smile. "Jaiston probably found something interesting and led them off on a merry chase. We should go find them before he gets himself in trouble again." The girl grinned at her mother's fond, yet exasperated description of her brother.

Her relief was short lived. By the tunnel they just came through, one of the three remaining guards gave a grunt of pain, his eyes rolling back into his head. A glint of silver pushed through his chest and pulled back. The guard fell to the floor in a heap. Everyone sat in stunned silence for several seconds before the man responsible for the guard's death stepped out from the darkness of the tunnel and the reality of the situation hit home. The children screamed and ran to the other side of the chamber. They huddled behind the adults with no way of escape. Unlike earlier rooms, this one only had two converging tunnels, and they were both within a few feet of each other. Both routes were effectively blocked by the monster and his two companions emerging just behind him.

The two guards stood bravely before their charges, ready to lay down their lives to keep them from harm, but they were outnumbered and outmatched. Both were quickly beaten and battered by the three invaders. Still, with every knock to the floor, they retook their positions and fought on. They got in good hits, but the monsters barely seemed to notice. They raked arms covered in bloody metal spikes over the guard's chests and backs. The first man punched one guard in the gut and followed with a hard swing against the back, to the sound of bones cracking. The guard went down. The remaining guard retook his position in front of them and held up his sword, ready to fight.

"Look at him," the monster taunted. "One man is going to take us all on." They laughed.

"Wrong," a voice called down the second tunnel. "There are two of us." A man rushed out of the darkness, cloak flapping with the speed of his movements. With a single strike, he took out one of the monsters. Taking advantage of the distraction, the guard attacked again, finally landing a killing blow while their rescuer finished off the third attacker.

The man pushed back his hood and Traelene gasped, running to hug him. "Kern," she said. "They told us you died."

He hugged her back and shrugged. "I'm here, now. The clerics' tree is only a short distance from here if you want to go there, or we could just wait out the battle down here."

"We must find Jaiston," Valesca said. "We were separated a ways back. One of the guards and the woman Samantha went back to find him, but they have been gone a long time."

"We'll find them," Kern promised solemnly. "Show me where you last saw everyone."

It didn't take long to get back to the chamber of many tunnels. Valesca pointed down the tunnel they came from, and Kern took a lantern to look around in the previous room. He returned quickly with the grim news of the other dead guard. Valesca felt her heart sink in despair. Keeping her face expres-

AMANDA YOUNG & RAYMOND YOUNG JR.

sionless, she held tightly to Emery and Krylena. They did not object.

"Where's Jaiston?" Krylena asked timidly.

Kern knelt in front of his niece, raising her chin with his knuckles. "Your brother is with a very brave woman. I once saw her defend a group of children she did not know, using her own body as a shield. She will keep him safe until we find them." He looked up at Valesca, and she felt somewhat comforted by his words.

"Look, Mommy, a stone," Emery said, pointing down a tunnel.

Valesca ran to pick it up. A stone, just like the ones Jaiston collected. She looked around. It was completely out of place here, not something that could have naturally fallen to the floor at this spot. "He went this way," she said with certainty, holding the stone tight in the palm of her hand.

"Then so do we," Kern said, leading the way.

———

THIS WAS A DARK NIGHT. Dim light from the magical sun over Merchant's Square barely reached the halfway point of the city. It was bright but localized. Over by the wall, she could see small specks of light from lanterns and torches. Perhaps she made the wrong choice, Mirerien mused. After hours of fighting, running between shops, shooting arrows from rooftops, and directing civilians to areas of greater safety, she was exhausted.

Thankfully, due to her brothers' efforts, the number of Cullers inside the city was not increasing, but those who remained were not the loud, boisterous brutes she spent a good portion of the evening fighting. They were quieter, scheming, and very dangerous. It took all of her concentration and keen elven senses to keep from being taken by surprise.

She heard a sound like chuckling or laughter and saw the shadows beside her move. A bush shook, and another shadow moved. The sounds of shuffling and laughter moved through the darkness, coming from several directions at once. She leveled her bow at the movement, but the creature jumped out and past her shoulder before she could shoot. She turned, trying to get a look at him, but he was gone.

Another laugh cackled behind her. She spun to face it only to be kicked in the side of the head by something small and green. It ran into the bushes before she could see what he was. Putting up her bow, Mirerien took out her hammer. She was an excellent shot with an arrow, but these guys were too quick for that.

Swinging around her hammer to get a feel for it and adjust back to that fighting style, she listened for a hint to where they were. "Over here," a voice said. She turned to the sound and was rewarded with a kick to the other side of her head. Mirerien massaged her neck and worked her sore jaw. Whoever these guys were, they enjoyed playing games, and one of them had a powerful kick.

The bushes moved, and she jumped back, too late. Expecting another kick, she did not notice the bolas until they wrapped tightly around her legs, bringing her to the ground with a painful thud. She swung from the ground at the shadowy figures jumping gleefully over her, just out of reach. Continuing to swing, she worked her feet loose. She threw the entangling weapon into their mix, hoping to at least knock out one. She couldn't be sure how many of them there were.

Mirerien felt a sharp pain at her shoulder and looked down. A fresh line of blood stained her shirt. She felt another one on her leg and flinched. They were escalating their little game. Rolling into the bushes, she attempted to put some space between her and them. Trees shook as they followed on either side. The leaves ahead of her shook, and she dropped her hammer through its loop and jumped, grabbing on to a low-hanging branch and swinging up into the trees. Running and jumping from limb to limb, she struggled to keep ahead of her pursuers, trying to buy time while she developed a strategy.

Though they were acrobatically inclined, few could catch an elf in a tree. Once they learned they could not catch her, they began throwing daggers at her feet. Each blade struck a little closer until one hit close enough to shake her balance. Slipping, she grabbed on to the limb, only to have one of the creatures land on the limb with a squat and blow a handful of sand in her face. Blinded and in pain from the sand in her eyes, she fell.

Lying alone in the darkness, unable to open her eyes more than a small fraction, Mirerien crawled toward the faint glow of moonlight. She closed her eyes gently and moved by touch, feeling as the ground turned from sand to stone. She heard their movement again and froze.

"Miri?" a voice called.

"Collin?" she answered, relieved to hear his voice and terrified for his safety.

She heard his footsteps and reached out, grateful for his touch. "You must leave here," she warned. "There are some kind of goblins, I think, in the trees."

"Goblins?" His disbelief was valid. As far as she knew, no goblins had ever been within the city's walls. Their lands were a great distance away, and they did not usually venture far from them. Not quickly trusted by other races, they were often attacked and rapidly killed once they left the protection of their homes.

"Yes, they are quick, but I saw one of them clearly just before he blew the sand in my eyes, and I fell."

"You were in the trees, here? The lowest branches are at

least fifty feet up. It's a wonder you survived such a fall. Here, tilt your head back."

She did as instructed and waited as he poured water over her open eyes. When he finished, she leaned her head forward, closing them again. She blinked a few times. The pain was still present, but it was manageable. She heard the rustling in the bushes and pushed Collin away. The cut meant for him sliced across her hand. She heard him curse and draw his blade. "No, stay back." She stood, pulling her hammer back out of its loop and closing her eyes.

"What are you doing? You can barely see."

"These goblins are masters of confusion, overwhelming the senses with misdirection. It is all lies." She felt one of the goblins strike and blocked his thrown dagger with her hammer. The air vibrated with his surprise and excitement. The bushes to her right rustled, but that was not the direction of danger. Swinging to the left, she knocked back two of the goblins who attempted to jump overhead. Eyes still closed, she felt the goblins, three of them, gather for a direct attack. Coming at her, they fought as one, a single entity with three heads and six arms, stabbing shots through the narrow spaces under their brothers' arms or by their sides. A normal fighter would stab his ally as often as his foe with such a technique. Again, it was a fighting style designed to confuse and affect their opponent. "I am Mirerien, Keeper of Order, Seer of Truth," she said, fighting their flurry of attacks with an ease she never before knew in battle. "Where I stand, there can be no lies!" She swung hard, knocking the goblins back into the depths of the forest. They rolled into the shadows, scurrying away into the darkness to look for easier prey.

Mirerien opened her eyes and dropped her hammer back into its loop. The cut on her hand was nearly healed.

"Should we go after them?" Collin asked, after a moment to register what he witnessed.

"No," she answered. "It will be over soon. Come, there is still much to do."

———

RAND WAS A MASTER RIDER. Lynnalin never truly appreciated how skilled he was before, but this battle dispelled all doubts. Expertly, he weaved in and out of the fighters, striking blows and moving on before he could be hit. His strategy was simple, cause as much damage and distraction as he could to take some of the pressure off the troops on foot. Many men were able to get in a killing blow while the Culler turned after Rand. Lynnalin provided cover for their run, protecting their sides and backs as Rand took stock of threats from the front.

But after hours of running, the hound was at its limits, and even Rand was hard pressed to push much more out of the poor beast. Lynnalin had long exhausted her trove of spells and many scrolls. Thank Venerith she still had her fire. From the look of things around the battlefield, the other mages were in the same position. She felt pity for the Alerian mages unfortunate enough to get caught on the ground. They did not have the fire to fall back on, and magic users were not known for their physical combat skills. Most who tried to fight by sword fell quickly.

She had little time to contemplate their fate as the hound fell suddenly, its leg twisted by a turn it was too tired to make. Both she and Rand tumbled off, separated by ten feet and a mass of fighters. Lynnalin jumped to her feet and was instantly thrown back down. Ground at her back, she pulled up her fire to guard against her attacker, but he did not shy from the flames. Instead, he struck through them. His blade dug into her shoulder and chest. Lynnalin screamed in pain, her vision blacking out for a moment. Her fire went out, but it didn't matter. It wasn't like it stopped him the first time. He raised his blade to finish her off, but before he could complete his task, a hammer covered in blue fire smashed into his jaw, sending him reeling back from the force. Rand continued swinging, giving the Culler no room to counterattack. With one last swing to the head, the Culler was dead.

Reaching down, Rand lifted Lynnalin from the ground and carried her away from the heavy fighting. Holding her with one arm, he fought with the other. Soldiers seeing them added their own aide. After all the times he helped them during the battle, they were glad to return the favor. Lynnalin struggled to breathe. The pressure on her chest was heavy. Putting her down behind the battered remains of a damaged cart, Rand bound her injuries as best he could. Given their location, it was difficult.

And so she lay, Rand fighting beside her, protecting her and himself with his mighty hammer. When she could, she sent out her fire, but otherwise, she could not move. Concentration lacking, even using the fire was not easy. She was sure she lost consciousness a few times. Then suddenly it was over. A horn blast rang through the air, and every single Culler stopped.

No matter where they were or what they were doing, they stopped like students responding to a bell calling an end to the school day. One man held aloft by the Culler he fought was instantly dropped. Even those lost in the battle rush, brutally beating their opponent past the point of resistance, stopped and simply walked away. Anyone who tried to stop them or continue to fight against them was casually pushed aside and forgotten.

Rand watched their departure with a mixture of relief and shock. That was quickly replaced by concern for her. Scooping her up, he ran through the stunned crowd in search of a cleric who still had healing magic left.

"Where are they going?" she gathered the energy to ask.

Before he could answer, the first Cullers made it to the wall and learned the startling truth. They weren't going anywhere. Lynnalin activated her last spell, a simple one to allow her the ability to see magical effects, and saw the glimmer of a magical barrier around the Square. Anyone who attempted to cross the barrier was thrown back. Quickly angry at the unforeseen impediment to their departure, the Cullers grew frantic, clawing at thin air, trying to escape. Others turned on the soldiers unfortunate enough to be near them. And so the fighting began again.

Ignoring everything else, Rand continued to search for a cleric. Lynnalin felt her magic fade, the shimmer of the wall disappearing. From Rand's worried face, she could only imagine how bad she looked. If it was half as bad as she felt, she could understand his urgency.

"Dwarf," she heard a man call. Rand stopped, and she saw King Eirae run toward them on his way to the wall. Pausing only briefly, he handed Rand two potions. "In thanks for the light," he explained. "Sorry it's not more, but that is all I have left."

"Thank you, Your Highness," Rand said gratefully, but Eirae was already running toward the fighting at the wall. Putting her back down, he uncorked the bottles and helped her take the healing potions. After the second bottle was empty, she still felt like a giant stepped on her chest and forgot to move, but it was an improvement. "How are you feeling?" Rand asked. His voice was laced with concern.

"Better," she answered honestly. It hurt to talk, but it was bearable. "You can go back to fighting. I'll be fine."

"Nah, I think I'd better stick around you for the time being.

At least until we can get you healed a bit more. Rest now, little wizard. You've done your part. I'll protect you now."

"If you insist." She knew better than to argue with a dwarf. Rand stood, still holding her close in his large arms as he continued to look for a healer. With the battle raging anew around them, Lynnalin rested her head against his chest. It felt good to have a dwarven protector, she decided. Very good.

————

THE SOUND of rushing water was a relief and a concern. She was parched and tired, but in the dark, the risk of somehow falling into the frigid water was great. Should that happen, they would be swept away long before they even knew where they were or what happened. Her shoe slipped on another slick rock, and she stumbled to catch her footing. Instead, she ended up falling into a cluster of rocks and adding to her wide assortment of bruises. "We need light," she said to herself.

"I can help," Jaiston said, pulling out something from his pocket. There was a small snap and the tunnel filled with light. Looking at her proudly, he held up his snapper light, a dried flower enhanced by magic. They were a children's toy, though admittedly a useful one. Each dried petal contained its own light spell. You had only to crush a petal to activate the spell. He still had three petals left on his.

"Thank you," she said, standing. The chamber they were in was curved around a window in the stone. Through the window, she could see the underground river. Lying on her side, she reached her arm in, pressing her shoulder up against the low ledge, and cupped her hand in the water, bringing it to her dry lips. "I don't suppose you have a cup in that bag of yours?" she asked.

"I have a rock that is bowled out like a cup," he said, pulling out the stone.

Samantha took the rock and scooped up some water, handing it first to Jaiston then taking the second cup for herself. Once they had their fill, she handed him back the stone and patted his head. "Let's get moving."

Feeling a rush of evil, she pushed the boy back just as a hand came swinging, throwing her against the wall. The invader held her there, his arm pressed against her chest, his elbow under her chin. His other hand held her loose arm in place. His body pressed into her legs. She couldn't move anything more than an inch before he clamped back down.

This man was far less mutilated than the invaders who sacked her home. He still possessed all his limbs, though he bore many scars. She felt his aura flicker, at first strongly evil. Then, as he looked at her, the nausea in her belly lessened. She looked in his eyes and saw a battle raging there. His aura flared back to evil, then softened again as his increased aggression caused her to flinch in pain. Whoever this poor man was, he still fought the sickness in his mind. Something of his old self remained, preventing him from finishing her off.

Concentrating, she reached out to the light spots of his soul, soothing and protecting them from the darkness surrounding them. His hold on her relaxed. Raising a hand slowly, she gently touched his arm and felt the negative influence on his mind wash away. His eyes cleared then filled with regret and horror. Stepping away from her, he fell to his knees and doubled over, crying, "Candice," repeatedly into his hands.

"Mother!" Jaiston called, seeing the others come rushing down the hall. Among them, much to her relief, was Kern. He walked past the man on the floor, recognition hitting his face as he heard the man say the name. "Are you hurt?" he asked Samantha, keeping his attention focused on them both.

"I'm fine," she answered. "I'm relieved to see you alive."

He smiled. "What happened to him?" He asked, still eyeing the man.

"He was ill. I could feel the sickness within him. When I touched him, I was somehow able to take it away."

Kern looked at her thoughtfully, then motioned to her sword. "That's a Paladin's blade you wear."

Samantha started. Paladins were holy warriors, defenders of the weak, protectors and bastions of goodness. To be a paladin was a divine calling, not a choice. They were renowned for their ability to fight evil. Some could even cure the sick. She looked down at her hand, the one she used to touch the man's arm. "Collin gave me the sword," she said, speaking quickly, nervously. "He said I reminded him of its original owner." She pulled the sword and sheath and held it out to Kern. "This doesn't belong with me. I'm no fighter. I am definitely no warrior. If anything, you should have it."

Kern put his hand on the sword and gently pushed it back. "Keep it."

"I don't even know how to use it," she continued to argue.

"You'll learn," he said confidently.

Reluctantly, she took back the blade, holding it in front of her chest like a security blanket. "What about him?" she asked of the man on the ground.

Taking a deep breath, Kern squatted by him and put a hand on the man's shoulder. "I know a girl named Candice," he said. The man looked up and fell silent. "She was a survivor from the raids on Breakeren. Her father saved her by sending her away on horseback. She is a very brave young girl."

The man began sobbing again. "My Candice, oh, my Candice, what have I done?"

"I can bring you to her," Kern offered.

"No!" he looked up in horror, moving away from everyone

in the chamber. "No, I can never face her again. I have done ... horrible things. No, it is better if I were dead. I should be dead." Turning from them, he ran off down the curved hall, into the darkness.

"Should we stop him?" Samantha asked.

"No," Kern said after a moment of thought. "There is nothing more you can do to help him. He must do the rest on his own."

The walls of the caves vibrated with a low hum. Everyone looked around in confusion. "I think that may be our cue to get above ground," Kern said. With no disagreements, they happily headed to the surface.

THIRTEEN

IT STILL HURT TO BREATHE. LYNNALIN FELT THE SCAR ON her chest and sighed. Looking out her window, she saw a city in celebration. Despite the damage left and lives lost, the people were happy to be alive. Taking her bag, she looked back on her room one last time and closed the door. Her room at the mage academy had been her home a long time, but it was time to leave. The headmaster was shocked when she told him. Everyone assumed she would continue her studies after the Queen's assignment. She was an excellent student and one of the more powerful wizards at the school or in the city.

But her heart wasn't in it anymore. She stayed so long because it seemed important to learn as much as she could. Now, very few things seemed truly important. She couldn't sit in a classroom and discuss magical theory while so much was going on in the world. She could still learn new spells and gain power on her own. After this long at it, she didn't need a teacher to show her what to do. Not only could she learn her own spells, she was on the verge of creating a few. No, it was time to move on.

"Are you headed to the river?" Rand asked, running up to join her on the sidewalk.

Lynnalin grinned at seeing him. After the night in the Square, he stayed by her side for three full days before he had to return to the stables and see about the remaining hounds. "No, I'm going to Bryce's tavern."

"'hat is quite a bag to carry to get a drink. Plan on staying awhile?" He fell into step beside her.

"Actually, I plan on leaving Suriax for a while," she confessed reluctantly.

"Need any company?"

"What about your hounds?" she reminded him, a little surprised by his question.

He waved off that argument. "I'll get my brother to watch them again. He'll hate it, but that makes it worth it right there."

Lynnalin laughed. Rand loved his twin brother, Larn, but they were dwarves and prone to rough dispositions. Rand's work with his hounds helped him learn a great deal of patience. His brother was somewhat lacking in that trait and preferred to do his own thing, avoiding the animals when possible. Rand took every opportunity he could to tease his brother about it.

"It may be dangerous?" she warned.

"No need to keep trying to convince me. I already said I'd go."

The cheers from the river drew their attention. Lynnalin looked at the crowd gathered to see a young guard receive accommodation and promotion into the military. His name was Camdon, a former flame guardsman, now a general. He led a group of the survivors they brought through the caves. Together, the men guaranteed the women and children made it on the last boat and then held the beach by the pier. Somehow, they survived the night with only a few loses. It was a miracle, and the story was told over and over throughout the city to raise morale and give everyone something positive to focus on. Although the men were from Alerian settlements, they had the respect of all Suriaxians. A few even expressed interest in remaining in the city. The others were split between those wishing to settle in Aleria and those wishing to return to the south and rebuild. Ultimately, Lynnalin thought the women, once they returned on the boats, would have a lot to say about where they all went.

"Have you talked to Zanden and Casther?" Lynnalin asked once they were past all the commotion.

"Yeah, I heard they're giving leadership of the army to Zanden. Once it is official, he's appointing Casther to a post under him, working with Sardon on training for the troops. They are both going to be busy for some time." It was a fitting reward. All three men were instrumental in organizing and leading the Suriaxian people in their resistance. Never backing down, until the last Culler stopped breathing, Zanden and Sardon fought the entire night and into the next day. Casther proved his own distinction after being separated by the magical barrier King Pielere somehow erected around the wall. Without the leadership of the men in the Square, he took charge, helping to funnel most of the fighting away from the residential areas, where many who were unable to evacuate in time remained.

"I'm surprised they didn't offer you a position." Rand's contribution in the battle was no less significant. He deserved recognition for his actions.

"Who said they didn't?" he responded calmly.

Lynnalin nearly gasped in shock. "Then, why are you leaving?"

Rand looked out in front of them and took a deep breath. "I had my fill of politics. It was bad enough just going on one assignment. I don't need to be under the queen's thumb all the time. The simplicity of the battle in the Square made up my mind. It didn't matter if they were attacking us or the Alerians. They were our enemy, so we fought them."

"So, you were already thinking about leaving?"

He gave a wink and a grin. "Have my hound saddled by the bridge. I was actually just coming to tell you 'goodbye.'"

"In that case, do we have time for a drink before we go? I'm buying."

"I never say 'no' to a free drink."

"What about your hound? Will he be okay so long without you?"

"Larn's with him," Rand informed her. "On second thought, let's make it two drinks."

———

NEVER HAD SO many people crowded into Merchant's Square. Suriaxians flooded into the Alerian side as they welcomed back the ships carrying those who evacuated prior to the fighting. It took nearly a week to find and kill every Culler who remained within the city walls. Kern worried there could still be more hiding somewhere. No one was really sure where all the rest went. In the early hours of the morning, before the sun began to lighten the sky, a horn rang out across both cities, heard even to the mountain passes where the evacuated ships sat waiting to return. It was the cause of the hum that shook the cave under the cleric's tree. At its call, all Cullers not trapped by Pielere's walls fled in all directions. Those trapped in the Square grew agitated to the point of absolute distraction.

Some people, especially in Suriax, continued to pursue and fight the monsters, but there were many people in need of healing and burying. Between the damage to the people and that to the buildings, there were plenty of other things to worry about. Most were simply glad it was over. Following so close to the destruction during the night of Blue Fire, Suriax was particularly hard hit, not that they would complain about it or accept any help.

The next boat let out its passengers to the cheers of the crowd. Kern watched from his perch in a tree outside the Square. The women and children he led through the mountains ran off the boat into the welcoming arms of their men, who were lucky to be alive. He still didn't know how they managed to fight and kill so many Cullers when they possessed very few weapons and no formal training.

Kern rested back on the branches and tried to remember the last time he took a break like this. Once sure his brothers' families were safe, he joined the fighting again to help root out any Culler who ignored the call to leave. From the reports, he was sure at least a few had snuck out after Pielere finally dropped the wall. He never did find those goblins Mirerien claimed to fight. Sleeping on rooftops and in trees, he searched every corner of the city from morning until nightfall with little break for anything else.

"You look exhausted," Pielere said, appearing by him in the tree.

Kern shrugged. "Just trying to make sure they're all gone before everyone goes back to their normal lives."

"I haven't felt any deaths in over a day," Pielere assured him. "And Samantha said she senses they are still near, but not in the city."

"Well, when you put it that way," Kern crossed his arms and closed his eyes. "I'm taking a nap. Wake me in a month."

"Don't you think you should talk to your friends first? They still don't believe you are alive. They seem to think we are in some kind of denial." He smiled.

Kern looked at his brother through one eye, the other one still half closed. "And what am I supposed to tell them?"

Pielere took a deep breath and paused. "The truth?" he offered.

"What are you guys going to do now, anyway?"

Pielere shrugged. "Continue to steward the law and see where that takes us." He looked off thoughtfully. "I feel we still have a little time before ..."

"Before?" Kern prompted when he fell silent.

"I don't know," he admitted. "Come on. You are missing the celebration." He patted Kern on the arm, his pain and fatigue melting away.

"Oh, alright, if you're going to do all that, I guess I have no choice."

Pielere laughed and teleported them to the gardens in the park by the large gazebo at the center of Aleria. People laughed and danced. Musicians played their songs. Despite the losses, they all knew how much worse it could have been and were grateful to be alive. Marcy and Thomas stood a few feet away, watching the celebration from the side.

"You know, you're a pushy god," Kern grumbled, walking toward his friends. Pielere chuckled behind him. Catching sight of Thomas' ears, he grinned. "Well, look at you two. I leave you alone for a week, and you go and get yourselves bonded."

"Kern!" Marcy cried. "It's true. You are alive. But how?"

"We saw you die," Thomas added, equally in shock.

Kern clasped his hands down on their shoulders and leaned between them. "Well, as it turns out, Pielere, Eirae, and Mirerien are gods."

They looked at each other, not nearly as surprised as he expected. Of course, there had been many rumors floating around the city since word of their unusual involvement in the battle spread. "That explains Frex," Thomas said, catching Kern completely off guard. Marcy nodded her agreement.

"What about Frex?"

"Take a look over there," Marcy motioned.

Kern looked to the people celebrating in the park. He saw the girl Candice dancing with Alnerand. They seemed to be having a good time. He was glad. He had not told her what happened with her father, and as far as he knew, the man had not reemerged. Maybe someday they would be reunited, but in the meantime, Kern was happy she was moving on and making new friends.

Beside them danced a young elven couple. They looked happy and carefree. The woman wore a simple white dress, accented with blue ribbons and sleeves. Her long, burgundy hair twirled around with her as they moved. The man danced with precision and skill usually only seen from older elves. Around his neck, he wore a woven green scarf. Kern stared. He knew that scarf. It was his uncle's most prized possession, a gift from his sister, Kern's mother. He looked at the man's face and knew this was his uncle, and he was happy. Kern laughed, feeling more hopeful than he had in years.

———

DEEP in the sanctuary of the mountains, nestled in isolated lakes separated from and fed by the Therion River by narrow tributaries, the refugee ships began their journey back up the river to the cities. They thought they were safe. If only they knew how close danger was, how close danger always was. True security was a lie. Safety and peace were a fleeting blip on the journey through pain and suffering. So was the way of the world.

Nadda watched them from her perch on the mountains,

north of the river. Her long hair whipped around in the strong mountain wind.

"It's time to go," Ridikquelass said, joining her on the ledge and whistling at the view. "Wow, how fun would it be to dive into the water from here?"

"*It is over a thousand-foot drop,*" Nadda pointed out, projecting her voice as she did, without moving her lips.

"I didn't say I'd survive it," Ridikquelass clarified, "only that it would be fun."

Nadda shook her head and pulled up her hair, tying it in a loose bun and letting the rest fall down. She put on her hat to cover the bun and hold it in place. With only the bottom portion of her hair peeking out, anyone who didn't know better would think her hair was very short. That was fine by her. The less people knew about her, the better. It made it easier to blend in and disappear when the need arose.

"It's too bad we didn't get our hands on those Alerian god-children," Ridik complained, her urge to jump off the cliff momentarily forgotten.

"*We acquired many new Suriaxian recruits,*" she reminded her.

"Yes, but half of them lost their fire trick."

Nadda shrugged. A hand came down on her shoulder, and she looked up at the massive being towering over them. "But," the man said in a deep, powerful voice, "those who did not lose the fire will prove a valuable asset to us. And you managed to convert a Sublinate as well." Ridikquelass beamed under his praise. Together the three of them walked back down the mountain to their waiting army.

DRAMATIS PERSONAE

a Glossary of Important People in Ondar

Characters Introduced in "Suriax"

Kern Tygierrenon - Brother of Alerian monarchs, half-brother of Queen Maerishka

Queen Maerishka - Ruler of Suriax

Three Lawgivers/Alerian Monarchs:
Eirae (the Punisher),
Pielere (the Protector),
Mirerien (the Keeper of Order, Seer of Truth)

King Alvexton - Human, ruler of the Southern Plains, married to Maerishka

Lynnalin Moesaius - Suriaxian elven mage, member of cinder unit

DRAMATIS PERSONAE

Zanden Fiereskai - Suriaxian, leader of cinder unit

Rand Vrock - Dwarf, marenpaie hound trainer, member of cinder unit

Thomas - Human, former Flame Guardsman, from the mountains

Marcy Kentalee - Full elf, Suriaxian, friend of Kern

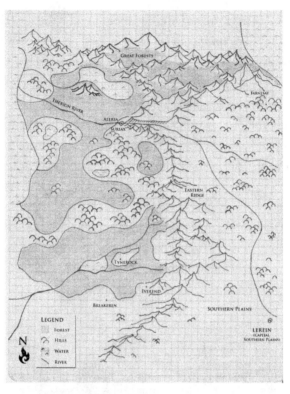

Aleria and Suriax are sister cities separated by the Therion River. They are connected by two bridges, one connecting at the center of each city and one connecting at Merchant's Square, an area open between the two cities. At the center of Aleria stands a massive park and gazebo, often used for weddings and other events of note. Just off from the park is the tree of the healing clerics. They are best known for their magic, which enables elves and non-elves to bind their life forces together in a permanent wedding ceremony.

Aleria is also well known for its theater, where impressive productions draw visitors from many neighboring lands. Homes in Aleria and Suriax are often nestled in large trees that reach up to two hundred feet in height.

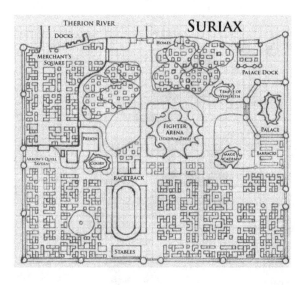

Suriax is well known for its fighter tournaments, such as the Tournament of Fire. It draws visitors from the far reaches of the continent. Suriaxians love to gamble and race marenpaie hounds in their large racetrack, near the southern wall of the city. Other areas of importance include the Temple of Venerith, located just outside the walls around the palace grounds, and the Arrow's Quill Tavern, run by Bryce Kentalee.

ABOUT THE AUTHOR

"What do you want to be?"

When I was little, I answered that question with actor, writer, artist, astronaut, singer, fashion designer, and a few other things. Adults would grin at my answer and say I hadn't made up my mind, yet. I told them, "No, I want to be all of them."

I never understood the idea of limiting yourself to one thing. Life is so big. There is room for many adventures.

As I grew, I continued to draw. I wrote and performed songs at talent shows. I drew out designs for clothing and even sewed some outfits. I made my own wedding dress by hand. I studied digital design and learned to do some basic work in photo programs. Friends will tell you I'm always jumping from one crazy project to another.

Again and again, I've been told what I was doing was too difficult, I didn't know enough, I could never do it. And every time I've plunged headfirst into whatever my passion was driving me towards with a near unwavering faith that I could do anything I put my mind to. People always want to tell you what you can't do. We are all capable of incredible things when we have faith and believe in ourselves. You may not succeed at everything you do, but you will never succeed at something you do not try.

Despite my vast array of different interests, writing has long held a special place in my soul. When I was twelve years old, I spent an entire summer writing a story. Before, I often started projects without finishing them. This was different. I wrote every day. I wrote in the car, my room, and the laundromat. I wrote until, just as vacation was coming to an end, my story was done. I finished it. I knew in that moment this was my calling in life. This was what I was meant to do.

From that moment on, I studied and wrote. Teachers and siblings told me to pursue a more practical career. I ignored them and followed my instincts.

When I needed a break, I still had all my other creative projects to help me recharge and have time to think. But I always returned to writing.

Through college, meeting and marrying my soulmate, working through jobs I hated, becoming mother to three wonderful boys, and homeschooling those same rambunctious boys, there have been challenges. There were times I've had to take a break from regular writing to care for newborns and sick children. Though, even when I wasn't actively putting pen to paper, (yes, I still use good old-fashioned notebooks and hand-writing much of the time) my books are always somewhere in my mind. I've spent many nights crouched over paper, using the dim light from my phone or a night light to see enough to put down my thoughts, while my children sleep a few feet away. Writing is who I am.

My passion is in paranormal romances and fantasy books. I love writing about werewolves, and other shapeshifters. I've also written about psychics.

I began writing fantasy after I was married. My husband and I used to get together with friends to play *Dungeons & Dragons* every Saturday. My husband wanted to create his own world with his own campaigns, so he enlisted my help in writing the background stories. He told me what his world was like and some of the key players and asked me to write backgrounds on other characters I told him what I had, and he added content or made changes to fit his vision. It was a lot of fun to work on this with him.

Later, I was looking for a quick project to write for NaNo-WriMo (National Novel Writing Month) and decided to put some of our notes into a full story of its own. That was the birth of our first collaborative fantasy book project. It is great to be able to share something that is such a big part of my soul with my husband. He has always supported my writing. Even when it hasn't paid off financially, he has never once asked me to stop.

I don't know what the future holds, but I know this is what I'm called to do.

Awake The Cullers
ISBN: 978-4-86750-296-9

Published by
Next Chapter
1-60-20 Minami-Otsuka
170-0005 Toshima-Ku, Tokyo
+818035793528

4th June 2021